Dancing with the Best Man

by

Robyn Rychards

This is a work of fiction. Names, characters, places, and incidents are either the product of the author's imagination or are used fictitiously, and any resemblance to actual persons living or dead, business establishments, events, or locales, is entirely coincidental.

Dancing with the Best Man

COPYRIGHT © 2019 by Robyn Van Matre

Cover Art by *Diana Carlile*

The Wild Rose Press, Inc.
PO Box 708
Adams Basin, NY 14410-0708
Visit us at www.thewildrosepress.com

Publishing History
First Sweetheart Rose Edition, 2019
Print ISBN 978-1-5092-2532-3
Digital ISBN 978-1-5092-2533-0

Published in the United States of America

"*Ai ai ai!* Icy cold and uptight on the outside, but those green eyes tell a different story."

With a gulp, she pulled the clip out of her hair, shook her head slightly and it tumbled down, falling to her waist. Could he discern the tumult inside her? Suddenly those green eyes couldn't look anywhere but at him as he pushed himself away from the wall and came toward her. He entered her personal space and all she could do was watch him as he picked up a strand of her hair.

"Amazing," he breathed as he rubbed the hair between his fingers. "If I hadn't seen those roots up close and personal, I'd find it hard to believe this color was real. It actually glitters, even in this weak lighting. I've never seen anything like it." His gaze roamed her face. "The pale eyebrows are a giveaway too. The only color to you are those pink lips, your green eyes, and the lovely rosy color you turn when you blush. Thank you for letting me see your hair in all its glory. Are you going to put it back up?"

"No." She shoved the clip in her purse as she continued to watch him.

"*Bueno,*" he said softly with a little nod. He let go of her hair, but didn't move away and the look in his eyes made her think of a drowning man desperately in need of a life preserver.

Praise for Robyn Rychards

Robyn has six books published.

~*~

DANCING WITH THE BEST MAN
won Chesapeake Bay Romance Writers
Rudy Award for 2016.

Dedication

For Kimberly Rowe.
Thanks for all your help, love and support
through the many drafts of not only this book
but all my others.

Acknowledgements

Special thanks to Joss Wood and Trish Wiley for your help and input on the story, to my beta readers, Telena Caldwell, Amanda Bagnall and Lori Merrill, and to Sherri Skanes for all things Hollywood and Los Angeles.

Chapter One

"Hold the elevator, *por favor!*"

A delicious-sounding male voice floated across the lobby as the elevator doors started to close, sending a completely unexpected—and unwanted—thrill down Jade Nichols' spine.

She would've loved having the elevator to herself for the ride to the hotel's restaurant on the thirty-fifth floor, and she barely suppressed a sarcastic 'Ha!' at herself. Riding an elevator alone in L.A. was a rarity. She jabbed the *Door Open* button as a man sprinted across the lobby and didn't realize she'd been holding her breath until after he slipped inside.

He pushed his hair back off his forehead, that errant lock the only indication his effort to catch the elevator affected him. "*Gracias.*"

"No problem. Which floor?"

He glanced at her out of the corner of his eye but remained facing the doors. "Thirty-fifth. *Gracias.*"

Again she experienced that unwanted thrill at the sound of his deep, softly accented voice. No need to push a different button then. They were both headed to L.A. Prime for dinner. She waited a moment for him to move away from the doors, to claim his own space, and was surprised when he didn't. It was a good-sized elevator, but still, it was an *elevator*. Space was at a premium, and he chose to stand right next to her?

1

Her space-bubble warning bells went off. She took a calming breath and got a whiff of spicy cologne mixed with a distinctively masculine scent. He smelled so damn good, it should be illegal. Or bottled for everyone to enjoy. It was compelling enough she almost stepped closer to breathe it in again. Instead she touched the silver, filigreed locket around her neck and moved to the back corner of the elevator. Hopefully, she prayed, returning to her personal space zone would aid in getting over this odd-for-her reaction to a close encounter with the male species.

As the awkward elevator silence continued, the electronic alerts that sounded as the car passed each floor couldn't happen quickly enough. Why did the restaurant have to be at the top of the Bonaventure Hotel? She shifted her gaze from the increasing numerical display to the man's rigid back. Expensive olive-green suit, over-long dark hair. Just as yummy as his scent and made her momentarily wish she'd taken a better look at the front of him when he dashed across the lobby.

Whoa...What was that about?

She didn't check men out. In fact, she never gave them a second glance. Her instinctive reaction was usually the exact opposite. Which had her giving him another look. A curious one this time. What was it about *him* that caught her interest?

Unfortunately, it didn't help her figure it out. It merely made her want to keep looking. Only this time it wasn't to enjoy the view—it was because he stood, board-rigid, in front of the doors, both hands balled into fists. She felt a twinge of sympathy and suppressed the urge to open his fists and hold his hand. She shifted on her feet and scrunched her brow. Now was not the time to experience such an untoward reaction. Mentally shaking her head, she looked down at her feet. It was the stress of the evening ahead. It had to be. Even though it was an evening she should be looking forward to. *Could they just get to the thirty-fifth floor already?*

Her sister was getting married in a couple months and had chosen her as the maid of honor. Her soon-to-be brother-in-law, Beck, was treating them to dinner at this upscale restaurant so Jade and the best man could get to know each other. Beck was doing all this out of concern for her, so she could feel more at ease about her part in the event. He didn't know anything about the true nature of her hang-ups—Jade made sure that was a secret Lexi never shared—but he knew taking part in the wedding ceremony was way out of her comfort zone.

Even without this little meet-and-greet session, Jade was determined her personal issues wouldn't ruin the wedding in any way. She was thrilled Lexi was marrying such a wonderful man. What she needed to do was enjoy the view her current companion provided instead of thinking about the number of times the best man might invade her personal space during the wedding and all the rituals accompanying it. Or if he would do it during dinner tonight.

Stop!

She took a deep breath. *Yum...*And found herself enjoying the view of the other passenger before she realized it. *So what? It was a perfectly normal thing to do.* The suit fit him well, showing off shoulders that looked strong and capable of carrying any load. Her fingers tingled, and she clenched her fist. Did she ever

3

want to run her fingers through his hair. *Was it as soft as it looked?* If nothing else, her companion was most definitely a good distraction.

The elevator coming to a shuddering, jarring halt between floors was not the kind of distraction she was looking for. She stumbled forward, he flew back, and they smacked into each other somewhere in the middle of the car. As she slammed against his hard, muscular frame, the air whooshed out of her lungs, and she nearly bit her tongue. Could banging into a wall have been any more painful?

The man swore under his breath in Spanish and spun so quickly he grabbed her by the arms before she ricocheted off him and hit the wall. Now she'd never know which was harder.

Completely muddled, she wasn't sure which was worse: slamming into a solid wall of muscle; hands grabbing her; the totally unexpected, completely disconcerting thrill of being touched. In any event, her knee-jerk reaction pulled her violently out of his grasp. Retreating as far back as she could into her corner, her cheeks felt like they were on fire. Not exactly the reaction she wanted to have, nor an impression she wanted to give. To anyone.

Terrific. She was behaving like an idiot in front of...

And that was when she *saw* him.

Ho-lee cow. Alejandro Rivera.

Not that she knew the guy personally, but she knew *of* him. Devil of the Dance Floor. No wonder he'd reacted so quickly when he grabbed her.

"You are all right, *señorita?*"

Perfunctory concern, judging by the expression on

his face and the lack of warmth in his voice. He'd displayed more emotion when he yelled across the lobby at her to hold the elevator.

She nodded, surprised she managed that much. Stuck in an elevator with *Dance Celebrity*'s superstar, Alejandro Rivera. What girl wouldn't be thanking their lucky stars?

Me.

Squeezing her eyes shut for a moment, Jade made a grab for the locket around her neck. Why, tonight of all nights, did she have to forget her purse in the car? If she'd remembered to take it with her when they first arrived at the hotel, she'd be sitting next to her sister enjoying a cocktail right now, rather than trapped in an elevator with a man who not only appealed to her in a way she'd never experienced before but was a celebrity to boot.

Pressing herself against the wall, she let go of the locket and looked determinedly at her feet, silently begging the elevator to start moving. She needed a moment to gather herself, and it better be a quick moment or Alejandro Rivera would know there was something wrong with her.

It felt like his hands were still on her arms. And it wasn't that yucky, get-your-hands-off-me-you-creep kind of feeling she usually got. The kind of feeling she'd endured too often. Her breath caught. Why didn't she feel that kind of panic right now? She always avoided casual touching to ensure she stayed in the present. Even more mind-blowing, it was the absolute flip-side of her normal reaction. This was a tingly, make your stomach somersault, scorch your skin kind of feeling she wasn't sure she wanted to experience.

Actually, part of her *did* want to feel it again, along with the rest of his perfectly sculpted physique. She forced herself not to think about that. It made those crazy sensations spread from her arms to other parts of her body.

She touched the locket again, resisting the urge to look at the picture of herself and Lexi inside. A quick peek at her companion turned into a gape of astonishment. With his forehead resting against the elevator doors, hands fisted at his sides, he was muttering in Spanish. After a few seconds of listening, and not feeling at all guilty for eavesdropping since she spoke Spanish, she realized he was *praying*. Desperately praying. The guy was hotter than all get out, and a dream to watch on television, but most definitely—strange.

Of course, with *his* reputation, bizarre behavior shouldn't come as a surprise. It was common knowledge he expected perfection from his dance partners and used some unusual tactics to get it, pushing until they met his standards. Not that she had any problem whatsoever with high standards.

After a few minutes, like he was waiting for an answer to his prayer and didn't receive one, he lifted his head and looked at the ceiling, took in a deep breath, then let it out slowly. Maybe it was some kind of Zen thing. Still, she needed to do something more than press herself into a corner and watch. She was *trapped* with him. It wasn't like she hadn't been around her share of freaks or more than her share of celebrity-types with major issues. She'd grown up in L.A. It was the up close and personal that was worrisome. If Jade was honest with herself, it was her desire to help him that bothered her most.

****

Alejandro Rivera swore violently to himself, then silently cursed the elevator, and the woman he was with. The last thing he needed right now was an audience. He drew deep within himself, tapping into every ounce of dance training he had to stop himself from banging his head on the door repeatedly. He wasn't five years old. He could do this.

Get a grip. Find a distraction.

When she spoke, providing the distraction he was looking for, he turned around to face her. "It appears the elevator isn't taking a momentary pause. We're stuck."

He nodded, and for the first time since he entered the elevator, actually looked at his companion. She felt *guapa* pressed up against him for those few moments when she stumbled into him. In fact, he'd be hard-pressed to remember the last time holding a woman felt so good. Therefore, her appearance came as a shock. He didn't go for blondes. He didn't go for tall and skinny. Dark, glamorous and curvy caught his attention every time. So what was it about her that made it difficult to look away? Certainly not the black dress that made him want to shudder. It looked like a sack hanging from her shoulders, and if he hadn't recently felt her up close and personal, he'd think she had no curves at all. And her hair…

Pulled so tight against her scalp, it looked painful. Maybe it was the concern shining from her beautiful green eyes.

She cleared her throat. "Um, are you okay?"

Concern for his well-being was mirrored in her

tone of voice. It made him wonder what his expression looked like. He bit back a sigh. Most likely it was his desperate attempt to stifle the panic. Had he prayed out loud? He needed to pull himself together. He didn't want to scare the poor woman. Being trapped in an elevator was definitely doing a number on him. He was *not* okay, but come hell or high water, he would pretend he was. If only he could get enough air. *Hell,* it was becoming an effort to breathe. He nodded but had to swallow to ease his dry throat before he could speak. He smiled, both for her benefit and his.

"You mean, other than the fact we're stuck in an elevator that isn't moving?"

She let out a small laugh. "Yeah. Other than that. You had a weird look on your face, and your color doesn't look too good. Maybe it's just the bad lighting in here. For a minute there I thought you were going to pass out. Or throw up. Which would not be a good thing. Being stuck in an elevator is bad enough. The last thing we need is the smell of vomit."

She bit her lip and looked at her feet. Maybe she'd recognized him and was feeling a little shy, or maybe embarrassed by what she'd just said? Regardless, he found it rather endearing.

"Oh hell, *no.* How humiliating would that be?" And how dangerously close he'd been to doing one or the other of those things. He chuckled so she would think he was joking, and she laughed along with him. He enjoyed the sound of it. It sent a little tingle through him which he enjoyed more than was probably good for him, though right now, it was the lesser of two evils.

"So…Do you think we should call someone, or wait a bit to see if it starts moving again?"

He checked his pants pockets and the breast pocket on his suit jacket before he remembered he'd misplaced his phone. "Might as well get people working on it as soon as we can. If it starts moving while we're calling, all the better. I don't have my phone with me. Do you have one?"

"I do."

She fumbled around in her purse for a moment before pulling it out triumphantly. His stomach sank when the look on her face turned to disappointment, but his lips twitched when she muttered a foul word. It seemed so at odds with her uptight, prim-and-proper appearance.

"You'd think I'd have learned by now to charge my phone before the battery runs out."

He shrugged. "At least you have it with you, unlike me. I have no clue where mine is."

"Well, it's good to know I'm not the only one on the planet who doesn't treat their phone like an appendage."

She looked at him and let out another one of those laughs, and he had the same reaction as before. Which he completely forgot about when he looked in her eyes. They sparkled with laughter. Actually sparkled, and were the clearest, most beautiful jade green he'd ever seen. He couldn't begin to count the number of women's eyes he'd looked into in his life and never seen a pair the color of hers. It was an effort to make himself look at something else. Not that there was much of a choice right now. Which brought him right back to how confined they were. He tugged at his silk tie and unbuttoned the top button of his linen dress shirt.

"Good thing the elevator has an emergency phone

then. We should use it."

"Indeed we should. Do you mind doing it? I think a plea from a woman might make them work a little quicker. You could even tell them you're stuck in here with a crazy man who's going to lose it if he doesn't get out soon."

Her brows pulled together, and her eyes flew to his face. "So you *were* on the verge of passing out or getting sick. Are you claustrophobic?"

Damn. He meant it to come across as a joke, but it looked like she wasn't going to fall for it. "No comment. Just pick up the phone and make that call, would you?"

"All right, already. Geez. Could you at least move out of my way so I can do it?"

She went from pressing herself into the corner to scooting along the wall, and he narrowed his eyes at her as he shifted from in front of the doors to the side of the elevator opposite the control panel. So he wasn't the only one here with issues. If he had to guess, based on the way she'd pulled out of his arms so quickly and how she was keeping her distance from him now, she didn't like people getting too close. Or maybe she was just afraid of him. Of being trapped with a man she didn't know. It could even be she was merely nervous because of *who* he was.

"You don't need to be afraid of me, *chica.* I'm not going to freak out on you, but I do rather feel like I'm suffocating, so the sooner we get out of here, the better."

He suppressed a desire to start pacing—the need to move so he didn't have to think—and leaned against the side wall of the elevator. His ears rang so loudly he couldn't hear anything else, which affected his ability to think clearly. He needed air. Why wasn't there any air in here? His heart rate quickened, and his breathing became labored. He closed his eyes and mentally began choreographing a new dance routine for his class of gifted students. It was something he meant to work on soon anyway because he needed something for an upcoming fundraiser. A much more productive thing to think about than praying.

It worked pretty well, too—until he heard the woman say the name *Lexi Nichols*.

No!

His eyes flew open, and he took a closer look at her. His jaw clenched. The family resemblance was undeniable. This had to be Lexi's sister, Jade. Maid of honor in his best friend's wedding. It was bad enough a stranger knew the secret he kept from everyone, but now that secret was known by someone in his orbit. All she had to do was mention his claustrophobia to Lexi, and he'd feel uncomfortable every time he was around them.

Was Lexi's sister the kind of person who would sell this story to the tabloids?

****

The man's reassuring voice on the other end of the phone calmed Jade somewhat. Since they might be stuck for a while, she asked him to let her sister know what was happening. She suppressed a growl of frustration as she hung up, and moved back to her corner of the elevator, her eyes on the lighted number over the doors, willing it to change as an indication the elevator was working again.

"How long will it take to get us out of here?"

She jumped at the sound of his voice. In her frustration, she momentarily forgot he was there. She looked over at him leaning against the side wall opposite her, and his compelling eyes snared her gaze. They were a beautiful, golden topaz, a remarkable contrast to his dark hair and bronzed skin. He reminded her of a sleek black cat with golden eyes. Not any feline…A black panther. All leashed energy and rippling strength. Watching him on television hadn't prepared her for the reality of looking into those eyes, and she was unreasonably irritated by the thrill his softly accented voice gave her again. Or maybe she was irritated because she was so over being stuck in an elevator everything bothered her.

"They couldn't really tell me how long. Just got a standard 'As soon as we can.' We may end up having to wait for the fire department to get us out if they can't figure out what's gone wrong." She took a calming breath through her nose. "Are you going to be okay?"

His eyes darted away, then back to her. He sighed. "Yes. I'm fine."

She found that hard to believe but took his word for it. Maybe it was her turn to start praying he didn't go completely bonkers before they got the elevator working again.

Deciding she might as well get comfortable, she slithered to the floor to sit cross-legged with her elbows on her knees and her chin in her hands. Maybe she should try and zone out like he'd done. Her companion may be a celebrity, but that didn't mean she really knew him, or trusted him. She was trapped with him and he could pull anything. Might even feel he had the right to do whatever he wanted with her because he was a celebrity. Men with power set her teeth on edge.

I hope you rot in hell, Gene Murray.

Her heart picked up its pace, and she grabbed her locket, ran her thumb over its bumpy, filigreed surface, pressing it down so hard it left an imprint on her skin. She could feel herself spiraling down, and hoped it would work its usual magic, ground her and keep her in the now. Goose bumps raised on her skin, and the feel of *that man's* hands touching her everywhere rose from the past and became the present. She closed her eyes.

Stay away from me. You have no power over me anymore. I'm strong. I got away from you, and I got Lexi away from you.

She opened her eyes, opened the locket, and focused on the picture of herself and her sister. The specter from her past vanished; the present returned and along with it, the calm she sought.

However, she didn't notice her companion had moved, making the panther analogy more apt. She was startled out of her skin when he suddenly crouched down in front of her, invading her personal space. Granted, her personal space area did take in a wider scope than the average person's. Then her eyes met a pair of fiery topaz ones, and she forgot everything. Those eyes gave her a once-over, lingering way too long on her legs—*she really should've worn stockings*—before returning to her face. It took everything she had not to squirm.

"Why don't we figure a way out of here ourselves instead of waiting on someone else?"

Chapter Two

"I think it's time we take matters into our own hands." He tipped his head back and looked at the ceiling for a few moments before turning his disturbing gaze on her. "I want to try to climb out through the ceiling."

"You're crazy. Even if I wasn't wearing a dress, there is no way I am climbing out of here."

"Maybe, but it seems to me what's really insane is being content to sit here and wait. C'mon, it won't be too difficult. I can lift you up with no problem. Then I'll pull myself up. I'm sure we'll be able to find a way out through the elevator shaft."

"Oh. My. God. You're serious." She shook her head. "Listen, this is not a movie. Climbing into an elevator shaft is dangerous. What if the elevator started moving again while we we're in there?"

She made the mistake of looking into his eyes. For a moment it was like looking at a scared little boy desperate to escape. The desire to take him in her arms and assure him everything would be okay came over her. Just like she did for Lexi after their mom died. This urge to comfort was such a foreign feeling to have for a man, she wasn't sure how to react. Regardless, she wasn't going to let the emotions make her do something stupid. Like climb out the ceiling of an elevator to make that look in his eyes disappear.

"We need to wait for the people who know what they're doing. The only way I'm climbing through the ceiling is if a fireman tells me to."

He narrowed his eyes for a moment. "Listen, I don't want to freak you out or anything, but here's something to think about. What if the elevator starts doing a free fall? Who knows what's wrong with this thing. It could merely be a computer problem, which they might figure out at any minute and we'd start moving again. Or, it could be a mechanical issue. In which case, there's no telling what other things might fail or how long it will take to find the problem before they call in the fire department to get us out of here. We're somewhere between the twentieth and twenty-first floor, if the display above the door is to be believed. That's a hell of a long way down to the bottom, *señorita.*"

She couldn't help but shiver at the thought; her stomach did an ugly little flip. She suppressed a sudden urge to grab his hand again, this time to reassure herself. Instead, she pulled her legs to her chest, wrapped her arms around them and rested her chin on her knees.

"If they really thought we were in danger, the man on the phone would've told me they're calling the fire department to get us out quickly. I think you're trying to scare me into climbing out."

He looked down at the floor for several long seconds before slowly bringing his gaze back to her face. "I will admit I'm pretty desperate to get out of here, but I'm not trying to scare you into climbing out with me. I am worried about these things I said. If it was only me, I would have tried to climb out already.

But I can't leave you here. I want you to be safe, too."

"Thank you for that. It seems we're taking a chance, either way, but I like my odds staying in the elevator."

He made a frustrated noise, and the lost-little-boy look returned to his eyes for a moment. Which garnered the same response in her as it did the first time. Her hands clenched around her arms to keep from grabbing his hand.

"Okay. For now," he said. "But if we're in here any length of time, I hope you change your mind. There's no telling what might happen if I stay in here too long."

She gave a nervous laugh. "Is that a threat or a warning?"

He stood, looking down at her. "Both. Great legs, by the way."

She looked down and thought she'd die of embarrassment. She forgot she was wearing a dress when she pulled her legs to her chest. She didn't usually wear one, and he had her thoughts so jumbled she didn't remember she wasn't appropriately dressed for such a sitting position. She returned to sitting cross-legged, making sure her dress was pulled down over her legs so only her feet, in the black stiletto heels which Lexi insisted she buy, showed.

She forced her gaze to remain on the floor and realized he was pacing when his stupidly-expensive loafers moved back and forth across her line of vision. Watching the shoes got old after a while, so she raised her eyes a bit. Big mistake. The flash of the diamond and platinum ring on his little finger and the chunky platinum chain that peeked out from his cuff distracted her for a moment from his tight behind and well-formed thighs. Not for nearly long enough. She couldn't tear her eyes away from that part of his anatomy. To the point she became disgusted with herself. Not that she hadn't ogled that part of him repeatedly while he performed. But this was live and in person. He might catch her at it.

On the upside, her past wasn't haunting her anymore.

When she felt the heat in her cheeks and her heart pounding so hard she'd swear he could hear it, she managed to pull her eyes away and glued them to the floor, waiting for his feet to move into her line of vision again. When they hadn't made an appearance for quite some time, she found herself raising her head again. He was leaning against the side wall at the opposite end of the elevator, his hands over his face, dark hair a disheveled mess, tie askew, his perfectly groomed look completely gone. Moving his hands from his face, he ran them both through his hair again, then crossed his arms.

Wow. Confinement really was getting to him. Maybe she should try and climb out with him. A man losing it because of claustrophobia might be more dangerous than climbing out through the elevator shaft. Was there anything she could do to distract him?

She stood. "You really are having a hard time." She winced. Not the best thing to say as a distraction.

He gave a self-deprecating smile. "I've never been trapped in an elevator before. I didn't realize it would be so hard."

"Your secret's safe with me. I'm not going to sell the story of what it's like being trapped in an elevator with Alejandro Rivera to the highest bidder. So that's one less thing for you to worry about. If you really think you're going to lose it, we can try climbing out through the ceiling."

"Ah, so you do know who I am. Climbing out of here would make for a much better story, but I don't think we need to try that just yet. I know something that might take my mind off things for a bit. Your hair has been driving me crazy. How about taking the clip out and letting it down?"

No, no no…Why did he have to go and give her a look like that? She wanted to come across as unimpressed with the fact he was *Alejandro Rivera,* and now she was afraid she might melt at his feet. She cleared her throat, at a loss for words. Right now, he wasn't the larger-than-life celebrity she was familiar with on the television screen. He was a man facing a fear he couldn't control, grasping at anything to help him cope, and she couldn't ignore his need, or the desire rising in her to do what she could to help him. It was the same kind of feeling she experienced trying to protect her younger sister when their mother was no longer around to look after them.

"*Ai ai ai!* Icy cold and uptight on the outside, but those green eyes tell a different story."

With a gulp, she pulled the clip out of her hair, shook her head slightly, and it tumbled down, falling to her waist. Could he discern the tumult inside her? Suddenly those green eyes couldn't look anywhere but at him as he pushed himself away from the wall and came toward her. He entered her personal space, and all she could do was watch him as he picked up a strand of her hair.

"Amazing," he breathed as he rubbed the hair

between his fingers. "If I hadn't seen those roots up close and personal, I'd find it hard to believe this color was real. It actually glitters, even in this weak lighting. I've never seen anything like it." His gaze roamed her face. "The pale eyebrows are a giveaway too. The only color to you are those pink lips, your green eyes, and the lovely rosy color you turn when you blush. Thank you for letting me see your hair in all its glory. Are you going to put it back up?"

"No." She shoved the clip in her purse as she continued to watch him.

"*Bueno,*" he said softly with a little nod. He let go of her hair but didn't move away, and the look in his eyes made her think of a drowning man desperately in need of a life preserver.

She grabbed his hands and squeezed them reassuringly. "It's okay. We're going to be okay. We *will* get out of here."

His hands gripped hers so tightly it was an effort not to wince. Or pull away in fear. This man needed her to *not* go crazy on him right now. She had to remain calm and keep her wits about her. Like the night she left home with a fourteen-year-old Lexi in tow, trying not to wake the sleeping predator they lived with. Again, but for entirely different reasons, someone was relying on her to be the strong one.

"*Si.* I know this in my head, but it doesn't change anything. Which is stupid and makes no sense. I should be the one making this better for you. Having control over my body is part of my job description."

"True. And you do an amazing job of it. Still, sometimes our mind can't control our body's instinctive reaction, so we have to find a new way to overcome that instinct."

She stepped closer to him so their bodies were almost touching. In fact, when she took in a deep breath, part of her body *did* touch his for a brief moment. Her heart pounded so hard she worried she couldn't get enough air to keep up with it. Oddly, it wasn't with fear but excitement—and the undeniable urge to know what it would feel like to kiss this man.

Her new way of overcoming her usual instinct to avoid intimacy? Maybe, but regardless, at that moment, she hoped it was a way for him to forget his fear. She let go of his hands, and tentatively placed hers on his shoulders, rose on her toes, and touched his mouth with hers. He was at the perfect height, so it didn't take much effort on her part to do it in a way that didn't require full-body contact. This wasn't the time to test out whether full-body contact would send her over the edge.

She moved her lips on his; when he returned the pressure, an unexpected thrill shot through her from head to toe. God, it had been so long since she'd kissed someone she could hardly remember how to do it. So it was a good thing he was quick to respond. To place his hands on her hips and show her what needed to be done. Did he instinctively know pulling her close was a bad idea?

Suddenly nervous—of what she was doing, of what might happen next, of who she was being so forward with, she didn't know—she ended the kiss, moving slightly away from him and dropping her hands from his shoulders. He was a little slower to respond, his hands softly caressing her before he let her go.

Still, she couldn't manage to break eye contact,

even though that lost little boy look was nowhere to be found. He was all man now; the heat of his gaze and the slight flush in his cheeks told her he enjoyed it. How stupid of her not to think things through. What would happen if he decided he wanted another deeper, more intimate kiss?

The elevator jarred, made a harsh noise, and finally resumed its upward climb. The sudden movement of it threw Jade back against the wall, and Alejandro stumbled toward her, pinning her with his body as he caught himself with his hands on either side of her head. Eyes like twin flames locked with hers and she was lost. Apparently this was one man who could invade her personal space, and she didn't have a breakdown. The shock of realizing she actually relished having his body pressed against her left her reeling. And completely unprepared when his mouth claimed hers. Without the least bit of hesitation, she wrapped arms around his neck and eagerly responded. She was encouraging, enjoying, *reveling* in all this physical contact. That rushing, dropping feeling of an elevator ride was nothing compared to kissing Alejandro Rivera.

It was only the abrupt stop at the end that brought her back to reality. And him. He jumped away like he'd been burned and spun around to face the doors as they opened. Exiting the elevator like a bat out of hell, he went straight to the men's restroom.

Jade exited more slowly and leaned against the wall next to the elevator. Not only did she need to recover from being trapped in an elevator, she needed time to pull herself together. She'd *liked* his kiss. *Enjoyed* the feel of his hands. Didn't want him to stop.

Plus, *she* kissed *him*. She not only enjoyed being

kissed by a man, she initiated it. Why *him*? What was it about *him*?

"Jade, thank God."

Lexi. She could've used a little more time to gather her wits before being social, but was it possible after a kiss which made her feel…all sorts of feels she never imagined existed?

"What great timing. I'm on my way back from the bathroom. Are you okay?" Her sister grabbed her hand, gave it a squeeze, then let it go. "What a nightmare! Were you in there by yourself?"

Jade knew she was asking more than the words implied. But it wasn't Lexi's job to worry about *her*. Although, the fact she didn't have to lie to her about it, that she really was all right, put the nerve-wracking experience in a better light. Who knew being stuck in an elevator could be such a life-changing event? For the first time she didn't want to share everything with Lexi. She didn't even want her to know it was Alejandro Rivera who'd been in the elevator with her. She'd ask too many questions Jade would rather not answer. Questions she didn't really know the answers to herself.

"I'm okay, though I'm not sure that would be the case had it taken longer for the elevator to get working. And no, I wasn't alone. A man was riding with me."

Lexi grabbed her hand again. The only person in the world who could touch her, and it felt normal. Scratch that. She'd initiated physical contact with Alejandro Rivera, and she suspected her reaction to him was a normal one for ninety-nine percent of the female population. *Why, oh why, did he have to be a celebrity?*

She just stopped herself from shaking her head at herself. She didn't need Lexi getting more worked up than she was, and if she thought she was shaking her head at her, Lexi would be all over it. So what if he was a celebrity. She was grateful to know she could have a normal reaction to a man's touch. Progress was progress, no matter how it happened.

So move on already. Tonight is about Lexi's wedding.

"Jade. Are you sure you're okay?"

And now her silence had alerted Lexi all was not right anyway, so she quickly nodded. "I'm fine. In a lot of ways better than fine. I handled the situation without falling apart. In fact, considering I was trapped in an elevator with a man, I did rather well. Which tells me the past is truly in the past." *Well, mostly...* "In fact, the guy in there with me handled it worse than I did."

Lexi laughed and gave her hand a squeeze before letting it go. "That's because you're amazing, Jade. By the way, I'm glad you decided to let your hair down. Now, if I could just get you to do it all the time..."

Jade groaned. "Lexi, you know it's much easier at work if I have it up. Much easier for a lot of things if I wear it up."

"If you say so, but you're not fooling me. You wear it up or in a braid all the time. Boring, boring, boring. You already know what I think of that dress, so I won't go into it again. You could be a knockout with very little effort."

Jade bit back a frustrated groan, and as the noise of clanking silverware from the dining room registered, her stomach growled. She wanted to sit down and eat, not discuss her choice in clothing. "Really, Lexi? Like we haven't had this discussion a million times already? I'm not sure I believe I could be a knockout, or that I even want to be one, but that aside, you also know why I don't have any interest in making myself glamorous."

"Yeah. Okay. And I know this isn't the time or the place to discuss it, but in my opinion, until you stop hiding behind ugly clothes and schoolmarm-hair, you aren't past it. Still, thanks for wearing the shoes. At least your legs look terrific." Lexi laughed and gave her a wink. "Now, 'nuff said. Tonight is about me. The next few months are about me."

Jade laughed along with her sister then and gave her a hug. "Don't I know it?" So Alejandro hadn't said she had great legs just to flatter her. She probably shouldn't like the idea of that as much as she did. "But you better be careful there or I may never wear these shoes again."

"God, you're such an old stick in the mud. You're too young for that, Jade. I wish you'd let your hair down and do something crazy just for the hell of it. Just once. Enjoy being young. Promise me you'll give it a try after I'm married and you have no reason to worry about me, or set a good example for me, or feel responsible for me anymore."

The elevator doors opened and Jade watched enviously as a laughing couple exited and walked by them on their way to the restaurant. Why couldn't her ride have been as uneventful as theirs, not the life-changing event it turned out to be? She bit back words which would let Lexi know she'd just done something insane with Alejandro Rivera and prayed her expression didn't give anything away. "I will promise no such thing. Besides, it's not like I haven't done anything crazy ever. Maybe you were too young at the time to remember, is all."

"Maybe. Maybe not. To what are you referring?"

"Jake. One of my boyfriends in high school. The one whose father owned that high-end car dealership."

"I remember Jake. I liked him. He did pick you up in some pretty cool cars. He never came across as wild and crazy, though. Maybe I was too young to notice?"

"He had his moments, but he always behaved himself around mom. Man, did he drive some sweet cars. We used to see who could drive fastest through Hollywood Hills."

Lexi raised a skeptical brow. "I find it hard to believe you ever drove over the speed limit."

"Believe it, kiddo. And I was always the one who won that contest. However, it was Jake who ended up getting caught by the cops. It didn't go over too well with his dad, and Jake broke up with me because of it. He said I was a bad influence on him, and that his dad wouldn't let him drive any more of his sports cars if he hung out with me. Guess he liked the cars more than he liked me. Or maybe he decided he was more interested in having a pretty girl to drive around instead of a number nerd who had more fun driving the cars than riding in them."

Lexi made a frustrated noise. "See, this is what I'm talking about. You have to stop thinking of yourself as an accountant with a business to run and embrace the fact you're a young, beautiful woman with a lot more to offer the world than filing taxes."

Jade resisted the urge to shift restlessly on her feet. Alejandro had been in the men's room quite a while and the last thing she needed was for him to exit while she was there talking to Lexi. "I *am* an accountant with a business to run, a tall, skinny one who could use several more pounds, especially in the chest area."

"With amazing, genuinely blonde hair, sexy legs, and the most gorgeous eyes I've ever seen. But I'm done fighting this same old battle. At least for tonight. Beck's been at the table by himself long enough. Let's go sit down. I'm sure you could use a drink after the trauma of your elevator ride."

Jade linked her arm through Lexi's and turned her towards the dining room in relief. "Don't I know it! C'mon, this night is about you, not me. Let's enjoy some delicious food and great company. You picked a good man, Lexi. I'm thrilled for you."

****

Alejandro stood over the bathroom sink breathing like he'd run a marathon. Thank God the bathroom was empty. His hand actually shook slightly when he turned on the tap, but cold water on his face helped settle him some. He focused on the vision of Jade's long legs to stop himself from thinking about the closet that haunted his nightmares. Or his mother.

Not going there. Not now...Long, long legs...

*Gracias, Jade...*It was working. He took a deep, calming breath through his nose and blew it out his mouth. Who would've thought such a nerdy, uptight woman would be such a distraction?

Okay, he had to be seriously messed up right now. Why else would he spend so much time thinking about a woman who was nowhere near his type? But, had he ever experienced a kiss so hot? Was it the contrast of her outer appearance that made it such a turn on? Or was it his perspective making it larger than life because it kept him from thinking about the worst hours of his life?

He turned off the water, grabbed a paper towel, and dried his face, then went to work repairing the damage he'd done to his appearance while he was in that steel coffin.

Years of forcing himself to ride in elevators, and some cognitive behavioral therapy, led him to believe he'd conquered the claustrophobia. He wasn't sure which was worse, that he had so little control over his behavior in a trapped situation, or that someone else knew his secret fear. It would've been a lot easier on his ego if she'd thought he was an eccentric celebrity.

Damn. He wasn't supposed to care, but here he was, back to thinking about her. He needed to get over this. She was Lexi's maid of honor, and in his orbit now. No way in hell he could act on these feelings. She was the kind of woman who would want more than he was capable of giving. Or wanted to give. Hopefully it was just the claustrophobia messing with his head. Or it could be he was so used to being the one in charge, the one in control, he didn't know how to handle someone else having it.

Pull yourself together. He was way beyond late to his dinner engagement, and they were probably going crazy wondering what happened to him.

Where the hell did he leave his phone?

Chapter Three

Jade took another bracing sip from her exotic drink. After letting the bartender know her favorite animal and favorite place, he concocted this ambrosia especially for her. The crazy part was, she loved it. Though tonight, as long as it had plenty of alcohol, she probably wouldn't care what it tasted like. Still a bit rattled, though she'd handled things with Alejandro Rivera better than she thought she could with any man, she didn't want Lexi to know how the—*incident*—affected her. It was Lexi's night, and Jade would not detract from it.

Good lord, she'd *kissed* Alejandro Rivera. And thoroughly enjoyed it. She didn't know if she should rejoice at a normal reaction she hadn't felt since high school or cringe at her stupidity. A celebrity of all people. *Really?* Maybe another sip would help.

Lexi looked at her in concern. "Glad you like the drink there, Jay-Jay, but maybe you should take it easy on an empty stomach."

Geez... What was going on with her sister tonight? Since their mother died, Jade had gladly accepted the role of taking care of Lexi. Was the responsibility of getting married making her feel like their roles were reversed?

"You weren't the one stuck in an elevator for half an hour."

"If you need it, feel free to order another," Beck offered. "I'm paying, and money is no object tonight."

"Thanks. I'm pretty sure I'll be taking you up on that. So what's the deal with the best man? I thought he'd be here by the time I returned from getting my purse out of the car."

Lexi put an elbow on the table and rested her chin in her hand. "I can't imagine what's taking Han so long. He's seriously late now. At least forty-five minutes." She turned her worried gaze to her fiancé. "He hasn't texted you yet?"

He shook his head. "Nothing. I'm starting to get worried. He could've been stuck in the lobby while the elevator was down, I suppose, and he *can* be late when he's working, but I've never known him to be this late without letting me know what's going on." Suddenly he sat up in his seat, and a relieved look flitted across his face before he smiled and stood. "Han. Glad you made it. Everything all right?"

As Beck shook hands with his friend, Jade saw a flash of diamond and platinum in her peripheral vision. *You've got to be kidding me!* As the best man took the vacant seat next to hers, she kept her eyes glued to her glass. *His* hand rested on the tablecloth next to her arm, *in her personal space.* There was no mistaking that ring or that brand of invasion.

Han was Alejandro Rivera?

Just shoot me now…

She'd played dueling tongues, not only with a celebrity, but with Beck's best man.

"Running late," he murmured in that luscious, accented voice. "Then unexpected problems on top of it. I'm sorry I didn't let you know. I have no idea what I did with my phone. I hope you weren't too worried."

"We were getting there, but it's all good now," Beck said. "Lexi's sister, Jade, actually got stuck in the elevator on her way up and only joined us a little while ago. I think we're all starving at this point."

She sensed him shift in his seat but still couldn't bring herself to look at him. Not yet. She focused on the bird's eye view of Los Angeles afforded by the restaurant's wall of windows. Mountains in the distance, twinkling lights barely visible in the twilight. She looked around the room, appreciating the calming aspect of the décor. Muted golds and creamy yellows contrasted pleasantly with the dark wood of the round tables and the upholstery of the chairs. Strategically placed pillars and the whole less-is-more style that focused on the view of the city. She returned her attention to her drink and looked at her glass for several long, drawn out moments before she decided she *really* needed another sip. Maybe she should drain the thing and get another. She watched the ice clinking in her glass as she swallowed the liquid courage, praying it kicked in ASAP.

"So this is your sister, Lexi? I finally get to meet the maid of honor."

There was nothing for it now. She was going to have to look at him. On the upside, he hadn't mentioned their adventure in the elevator. Was he afraid she'd let on about his claustrophobia? She sat up straighter in her chair and clenched her teeth as she turned her head in his direction.

Whatever he'd done in the bathroom for the last fifteen minutes, it had worked wonders. The disheveled mess was completely gone. He had everything under control now, and when her eyes met those simmering topaz depths, she just *knew* he was thinking about their kiss. She ground her teeth together before making a deliberate effort to relax her jaw.

"Hello, Han. It's nice to finally meet you. Lexi never mentioned you were the famous Alejandro Rivera."

She fingered her locket for a moment. It was a relief when Lexi spoke up, giving her a reason to tear her gaze away from a man she liked looking at more than was good for her.

"I was worried it would freak you out too much," Lexi admitted. "I didn't want to scare you away from being in the wedding. You're committed now, Jay-Jay. No backing out allowed."

"Lexi, I'm happy to do whatever you want me to, you know that."

With a nod, her sister smiled slightly. "I do. I don't know that it's always a good thing. But I thought I'd save you some stress and worry, leaving it until just before the wedding to tell you. You're not mad, I hope."

"No. I appreciate the sentiment."

"Maybe she was just saving the best for last." Han's bright gaze never left her face as he took her hand and raised it to his lips. "*Hoye, chica.* The pleasure is mine, Jade."

Seriously? She was actually on the receiving end of his signature gesture. The one he gave his dance partner at the end of every performance. She let her hand lie limp in his grasp. No mean feat, but she wasn't about to become one more female who fell under his spell. She fluctuated between longing to keep her hand in his forever and the auto-pilot reaction to avoid all human contact. Somewhere in between was the response she wanted, but at this exact moment had a hard time determining what that was.

When his lips touched her knuckles, the jolt that ran up her arm had part of her wanting to run screaming from the room. The other part wanted him to kiss more than just her hand as she remembered what those very same lips felt like when they caressed her mouth. She stiffened, stifled a moan, and in an effort to ignore both impulses, attempted to glare at him. *Big mistake.* His eyes crinkled at the corners; the topaz color turned fiery yellow. Rather than end the salute to her hand, he opened his mouth and gave it a quick taste with his tongue.

She sucked in a hissing breath, sat up straighter, and willed her hand to remain limp with all she had. Her other hand fisted in her lap as she fought the desire to beg him to taste more of her, for his lips to travel up her arm until they were on her mouth, as they'd been less than an hour ago. It was imperative she stifled this unfamiliar longing to touch and be touched by him, and her fingernails digging into her palm did help.

"At least one of us is getting something out of it then. Can I have my hand back now?"

"Of course. The contrast between your skin and mine had me fascinated for a moment. Forgive me." As he let it go, *finally,* his gaze lowered and lingered a tad too long, before taking in the rest of her. He raised one brow then turned his attention back to Lexi and Beck.

She looked down to fiddle with the napkin in her lap. Arrogantly sure of himself, the Devil of the Dance Floor was out in full force. Of all the men out there, why did *he* have to be the one to bring an attraction to the male species roaring to life inside her? Her therapist had told her all along what she needed was for the right man to show up. It looked like that was money well-spent, but at the moment she wasn't as glad about it as she should be. She reached for her glass, hoping the alcohol would calm the maelstrom inside her.

In her frantic effort to recover from her latest encounter with *Han*, she had no clue what the conversation was about when she tuned in, but realized she missed something big when Lexi looked at her with eyes full of regret before returning her attention to Han.

"That's an awesome offer. We really appreciate it, but I'm not sure Jade wants to do something like that. Maybe just the wedding couple dance?"

"Wait a minute, Lexi," Jade said. "I missed something. What is it I don't want to do?"

"Good grief, Jay-Jay, I think you've had more than enough to drink." She let out a little laugh at her own joke. "Han offered us dance lessons as a wedding gift. He's going to choreograph our wedding dance and teach it to us, as well as do one for the wedding party. I know dancing isn't your thing, so I was telling him we don't have to do a special wedding party dance."

Once more, Jade looked down at her lap. Her hands were clenched into fists. Again. She squeezed her eyes shut and wished away the next two months.

"Ahh…*Sí.*" Han looked at Jade with a raised brow. "You don't like to—*dance.*"

He knew she didn't like having her personal space invaded, but she didn't want him to know the extent of her problem. Much less that he was the first one to be an exception.

Past problem. Hadn't the elevator ride proved how far she'd come since she was seventeen?

Pasting a smile on her face, she looked at her sister. She didn't want to think about the consequences, but he was *not* going to get the better of her. "Lexi, I want your wedding to be perfect, you know that. If it means choreographed wedding dances, I want to make it happen. Don't worry, I'll be fine but—" She attempted a smile. "—if we find out I have two left feet, it may not be as great as you'd like."

She buried her face in her drink, hoping the attention would shift from her while she got used to the idea. She loved dancing. She loved the idea of having special dances as part of the wedding. It would make her sister's day even more special. It was generous of Han to make the offer.

Next thing she knew, an arm draped across the back of her chair. He leaned in and whispered in her ear, "No one has two left feet when I'm done with them. Rest assured, our dance will be perfection, *chica.* To start with, the personal space bubble has got to go."

She turned her head; their noses almost touched. She *so* wanted to lean as far away as possible, but she refused to give him the satisfaction. She may not like the reason she didn't run screaming from the room at his proximity, but she was grateful for it in that moment.

Instead, she said, just loud enough for him to hear, "I *like* my personal space, and there's no reason for you to be in it right now. You need to remove your arm."

He traced a finger along her arm near where his hand rested on the back of her chair and laughed softly in her ear. "Remember, I know how much you enjoy having me invade your personal space, though I have a feeling you don't want your sister to know about that. I think we're keeping secrets for each other, aren't we?"

So they each had something on the other. Impasse. Still, she didn't need him in her personal space *right now*. "Han, none of this is about us. It's about Lexi and Beck. Let's keep it that way."

After he removed his arm, it took all her concentration to release her breath slowly rather than in a sigh of relief. Any kind of relationship with the man which didn't revolve around the wedding was out of the question. She had no interest in being one of his here-today-gone-tomorrow girlfriends, no matter how much she liked having him up close and personal. For all she knew, he could be acting interested right now as part of his Devil of the Dance Floor persona. She certainly wouldn't take the way he'd acted towards her in the elevator seriously. He probably would've done anything he could to cope with his claustrophobia. Including climb through the ceiling of the elevator.

Or kiss a woman he wasn't attracted to.

****

What was it about Jade Nichols that made him desperate for her attention, no matter how he got it? She knew his deep, dark secret. If he was smart, he'd be more careful. One word from her and it wouldn't be a secret anymore. Of course, it helped that she didn't want her sister to know they'd been stuck in the elevator together. Otherwise, *that* would've been the topic of conversation when he arrived at the table. The loss of control he felt in the elevator no longer plagued him. Her silence on the matter was evidence he could trust her with his secret. Which gave him back the control he craved. His life revolved around control, and he had every intention of keeping it that way. Control over his body, control over his dance partner, control over his future, control over his emotions. It served him well when he was young and got him where he was today. Light years away from the homeless boy who grew up on the streets of San Juan, Puerto Rico.

Every time he looked at her his head filled with a vision of those long, creamy, exquisitely shaped legs. He actually tried to look down her dress before he realized he was doing it. The back of his neck heated at the thought, and he pulled at his collar. He was hard-pressed to remember the last time he'd been so rude and disrespectful. Like his eyes had a mind of their own and were desperate to see every inch of her. He felt the same in the elevator when she pulled her legs to her chest and gave him a tantalizing view of delectable skin. It took everything he had to look away and act like he didn't want to strip off that ugly black dress of hers and see what she really looked like. Granted, he was totally a leg man; they'd held a fascination for him since he started noticing the opposite sex. So it didn't help that Jade Nichols had perfect dance legs. *Hell*. His breath quickened when he realized he'd be spending the next several weeks watching those legs, teaching them to dance, *touching* them.

He shifted in his seat. Not his first uncomfortable moment since Jade Nichols entered his orbit. Undoubtedly not the last either. Her obsession with keeping her personal space intact only made him want to invade it at every opportunity.

But *why*, for god's sake? What was so different about her? Normally a woman with...*quirks*, or for that matter one who wanted more than a good time, had him running a mile, because he didn't do emotional involvement. It wasn't worth the pain.

Was it because she wasn't enamored by him like most of the women he encountered? Or that she had no problem giving him what for? Was it the challenge of winning her over? For all of five seconds he settled on that one. Until it hit him straight between the eyes it was way more than that. He had no idea what her real issues were, but no doubt they revolved around her vigilant defense of her personal space. He'd done a good job of helping her with it in the elevator, too. She'd taken his hands; she'd kissed him. Which didn't explain why she was now playing the ice queen and didn't want him near her. The contradictions intrigued him. He was in *big* trouble.

As they waited for their meals to arrive, she talked to her sister, and he couldn't stop his gaze from roaming her face, fascinated despite himself. For all her lack of color and style, there was something about her that attracted him. A unique beauty he'd never encountered before. Personally, he loved color, which was why blondes never did it for him. After meeting Jade, he decided he might've been overlooking something amazing.

She wore no makeup, so the lack of color in her skin and hair made the color of her eyes and lips all the more vibrant. Having grown up around the theater business, he knew adding some color with makeup could be stunningly effective. She glanced down for a moment; her eyelashes were incredibly thick and long. He just hadn't noticed them before because of their pale color. If fate hadn't forced him to take a second look at this fascinating creature, he realized he would have missed out on something quite amazing.

Her fingers fiddled with her silverware and it drew his gaze as she returned her attention to her sister. He had no clue what they were talking about nor any interest in taking part in the conversation. At the moment, he had an overwhelming need to touch. To still the restless movements of those fingers. Even better, to feel them fiddling with *him. Hell*...

He brushed his fingers across the rich linen of the tablecloth, savoring the feel of it for a moment, but it failed to curb his desire to feel her skin, so he covered her hand with his. Instantly it stilled. Impressive. She did the same thing the last time he held her hand. Every other part of her went rigid, but the hand, completely limp. The muscle control it took to do something like that...He could hardly wait to see what she could do with that control on the dance floor.

He knew it was merely an excuse to touch her, but he justified it by telling himself she needed to get used to being close to him. The sooner that happened the better. He picked up her hand and cradled it between his. Hers fingered fluttered for a moment to get free, then stilled when her eyes met his.

"Relax and enjoy the evening, Jade," he said, soft enough the murmur of the surrounding diners kept Lexi and Beck from hearing him. "I'm happy for the opportunity to get to know you better; I hope we can be friends. When these two important people in our lives get married, we're going to be spending some time in each other's company. It's in everyone's best interests that we get along. I promise to do my best to make the dance lessons enjoyable."

He flashed her a charming smile and let go of her hand, not liking the odd little ache it left in his chest. Draping an arm along the back of her chair, he reclined in his seat as a waiter set his main course in front of him.

Once everyone was served, and the waiter disappeared, Han removed his arm, forcing his body to listen to his brain, and dug into his food. With his arm gone, he noticed her relax and eat her steak. After several sideways glances as he ate his salmon, which he didn't really taste he was so focused on *her,* he fought the desire to stop eating altogether and just watch. The way she closed her eyes and chewed slowly made his heart pound in his chest for a few beats. Once she swallowed the bite, she quickly took another and savored the taste again. He'd never seen a woman eat with such enjoyment. Or realized it could be so sexy when someone wasn't deliberately trying to make it so.

She set down her knife and fork on her plate with a clatter, turned towards him and demanded under her breath, "What?"

"My apologies, Jade. I didn't mean to make you uncomfortable."

He longed to run a finger down her cheek, hardly able to resist the need to feel her skin. She glanced at him quickly, and her cheeks turned pink. Her lashes fluttered for a moment before she returned her attention to her food. Was she as affected by him as he was by her? Or was it merely the effect he had on most women because he was a celebrity? Damn, he hoped not. For some reason he wanted more than something so superficial from her. *No, he didn't.* This was just a weird physical thing. That was all. She was a woman he was going to be around for years to come as his buddy's sister-in-law. Involvement with her, either emotionally or physically, could really screw things up.

"I am fascinated with how much you are enjoying your meal. I don't think I've ever seen a woman get such a thrill from eating."

"Then I guess the evening is filled with novel experiences for both of us."

He fought another smile as he impaled a piece of fish with his fork. He enjoyed how she treated him like a regular guy. *Had he ever been treated that way?*

He swallowed his bite. "Indeed…So Jade, what do you do for a living?"

As she savored a morsel of loaded baked potato, he momentarily forgot his question. His throat suddenly dry, he took a drink of water and ended up choking on it when she replied.

"I own an accounting firm." As she watched him recover, she continued, "Does that surprise you?"

He cleared his throat one last time. "No. You're definitely the accountant type. Plenty uptight enough, and I'm sure your numbers add up every time. Just swallowed wrong." *Could he make more of a fool of himself?* "Your name is rather descriptive. Did you come up with it yourself?"

She looked annoyed. No doubt he wasn't the first one to remark on it. "You mean 'Nichols' because I'm an accountant or 'Jade' because of my eyes? No. All mine from birth."

"Jade matches the color of your eyes perfectly, so what a nice coincidence. It makes it easy for people to remember."

The look in her eyes might have felled a lesser

man, but he expected it. Even enjoyed it. He did wince when she threw her napkin on the table, stood and grabbed her purse, and bit the inside of his cheek so he didn't say something to make her feel worse. He should've left her alone to enjoy her meal and the time with her sister.

So why hadn't he? Because she didn't throw herself at him like most women? Because he wanted to make her forget how needy he was in the elevator? *Grow up, Rivera. She deserves better.* He bit back a sigh. The way he fell apart in the elevator was so humiliating. He squirmed in his seat as he thought about it. Still, no excuse.

"I'm going to the restroom," she said in a frosty tone. "If you'll excuse me?"

Once she was out of earshot, Beck said, "Good God, Han, what is wrong with you? I've never seen you act like such an ass before. I don't want problems between you and Jade ruining our wedding."

Lexi laid a hand on Beck's arm. "I wouldn't worry too much, sweetheart. Jade wants our wedding to be perfect more than I do, I think. Like I said before, we don't need to have a wedding party dance if it causes too many problems."

"No, Lexi," Han said. "Beck's right. I'm being an ass. Since Beck has been like family to me and I think of him as a brother, I feel like you and Jade will be my in-laws. I want us to spend many happy years together; so far, I'm not doing a good job of it. Suffice to say, my head is a mess right now and it has nothing to do with Jade. Just some personal stuff I'm not handling very well at the moment."

Beck smiled and shrugged. "Hell, man, it's okay. Is

that why you were so late tonight?"

Han cleared his throat and again shifted in his seat. "Basically. Which means I'd already started the evening off on a bad note. I'm sorry, *ese.* Hopefully I can do better now I've got some food in my stomach."

Beck chuckled. "A man with an empty stomach is never a good thing, and speaking from experience, I know how grouchy you can be when you're hungry. It probably has something to do with all the calories you burn off on the dance floor."

"*Si.* And lunch was a long time ago."

Was his hunger combined with being trapped in the elevator why he wasn't himself tonight?

****

Jade knew she'd been in the ladies' room too long, but each time she started to leave, she lost her nerve. Just the thought of going back to the table made her quiver. She feared Han would put his hands on her again and wasn't sure how much longer she could pretend she didn't care. Since she *knew* he was doing it deliberately, she was all the more determined not to react. At this point, though, it had taken its toll, and all the relaxing techniques in the world weren't going to fix her problem.

Eventually, she accepted she couldn't put off her return any longer. Only to fight the urge to turn right back around and run away. The table was empty but for…Alejandro Rivera.

The man was put on this planet for the specific purpose of torturing her, she just knew it. Where were Lexi and Beck? Since her sister hadn't joined her in the restroom, she had a sinking feeling they'd abandoned her to the Devil of the Dance Floor. She threw back her shoulders, clenched her jaw and marched over to the table. Time for her to go home.

Oh God, no! She came with her sister. Who wouldn't leave without her, so they had to be around somewhere. She let her breath out slowly in an effort to calm down.

The waiter held out her chair out for her, so she couldn't scoot it away from Han. Why couldn't the table be square rather than round? She did manage a bit of a sideways maneuver as she scooted it in, putting a little more room between them, which made her feel a bit better.

She finished off her drink before asking the obvious, "Where are Lexi and Beck?"

Han swallowed the last of the water in his glass and as he set it down, a delicious concoction of a dessert was placed in front of her. Suddenly, the fact she was alone with a man who made her feel all sorts of things she didn't want to feel was forgotten. Eagerly, she grabbed her fork and dug in.

"She got a migraine and Beck took her home. I said I'd give you a ride to your house, so they could leave right away." A smile tugged at his lips as he watched her. "I figured you wouldn't want to miss out on the dessert, considering how much you enjoyed the main course. Lexi ordered it for you. Crème brûlée cheesecake."

Jade moaned as the heavenly flavors of the gourmet treat exploded on her tongue, and she forgot her issues with Han. "You have *got* to try this. I'm going to be spoiled for life after eating this epicurean delight."

With a shrug, he picked up his fork and tasted his.

Jade made the mistake of looking over at him just as his tongue darted out to grab a piece stuck to his lip. She was *not* going to think about what that tongue had done to her, so she frantically shoveled another bite in her mouth. More than anything *she* wanted to be the one licking the most delicious dessert she'd ever tasted off the most delicious *lips* she'd ever tasted. Still, as desperate as she was to get away from this guy, there was no way she was leaving before she finished every mouth-watering bite.

It wasn't until she sat back in her seat with a groan, her stomach so full she was afraid it might burst, that she remembered there was still a ride in the elevator to get through.

"Eat too much?"

She gave him a dirty look, and his amused chuckle shouldn't have annoyed her. Wiping her lips with her napkin to hide her expression, she told herself she'd be home alone soon. She was just overly stressed from the events of the evening. With sleep and some alone time, she'd be fine. Half hour more, tops, and she was home free. It was herself she was frustrated with more than anything, and it wasn't fair to take it out on Han. He had no control over how her body was reacting to him. Most likely he was a spoiled celebrity used to getting whatever and whomever he wanted when he wanted it. Her refusal to give him that was probably egging him on. Especially since *she'd* kissed *him* in the elevator.

He threw his napkin on the table. "Ready to go then? Beck paid the bill, so we're free to leave whenever you like."

"Mostly ready. Just mentally preparing myself to get back in the elevator. It's not an experience I care to repeat at the moment."

He stood, and she quickly did the same. Grabbing her purse, she slung it over her shoulder and headed toward the exit. She didn't realize how closely he was following her until he spoke.

"It's an experience I have no intention of repeating, and since I have no reason to look like I'm okay with it for you, I'm taking the stairs."

That stopped her in her tracks, and he slammed into the back of her, his hands descending on her shoulders to steady them both. He remained motionless for a long drawn out moment, then bent his head and whispered in her ear, "Mmmm…*Guapa*."

His voice in her ear sent shivers straight to her toes, and her heart started to pound in her chest. "Now *this* is my kind of dessert. You have no idea how much I'm looking forward to our dance lessons."

She clenched her teeth in order to resist the urge to melt into him and tried to pull away instead. "If you don't let go *now*, I'm going to cause a scene the tabloids will love."

He removed his hands with a chuckle, running a finger down her arm from shoulder to elbow before backing away. "I've had enough of those for one evening, even if it was a private one in an elevator. So, are we planning on standing here for a while or what?"

With a shake of her head, she started moving again. "I'm taking the elevator. I'll meet you in the lobby."

"Okay."

He bobbed his head in acknowledgment and strode to the stairwell while she went to the bank of elevators and pushed the call button. However, when the doors opened, and she was faced with the prospect of being closed in that small space again, she couldn't bring herself to do it. She let out a resigned sigh. The evening had taken its toll, and she didn't have it in her to face a ride in an elevator right now. She didn't relish the idea of barfing her delicious dinner all over the elevator and anyone who happened to be in it with her. It would have to be the stairs. She wasn't sure about walking all the way down on a full stomach, but at least Han had a head start, and she'd have some time to herself.

That dream world lasted all of five seconds. When she turned toward the door to the stairwell, there he stood, holding it open for her with a mocking lift of his brow.

"Bit much at this point, isn't it?" He swept out a hand dramatically. "After you, *chica.*"

Flouncing past him, she started the long trek to the first floor.

Chapter Four

They made it down three flights in blessed silence, the only noise the echo of their footsteps. As far as Jade was concerned it wasn't near long enough before Han spoke. Not that his voice itself irritated her, rather, it was her reaction to it. No matter the words, the sound of them turned her insides to goo. It must be the Spanish accent. Not strong enough to make him hard to understand, but enough to deliciously flavor every word.

"Owning your own accounting firm is pretty impressive. How did you manage it at such a young age?"

"It's a long story." She wasn't sure she wanted him to know her life story, so she hoped he didn't push it. "How young do you think I am?"

"I know Lexi just graduated college a year ago, so I'm guessing you're a year or two older."

"Try six."

He shrugged a shoulder. "So I was off a few years. Late twenties instead of mid. I've got a good four years on you."

She blew out a breath. "Listen, you don't have to be polite and walk next to me; I'm sure my pace is slower than you'd like. Go at your own speed, and I'll meet you at the bottom."

"That's okay. I'm good."

Well, that didn't work. Time to try good old honesty. Though the thought of opening up to him made her cringe. She stopped, a hand on the railing, and he was two steps further down when he came to a halt. She swallowed, and her voice came out at a slightly lower octave than normal. "Han, I've reached my limit here. I really need you to give me some space." *Please don't ask why.*

She had no clue what to tell him, but it wouldn't be the truth. That she didn't like how much she liked being near him. That *any* man could have such an effect on her. Or that this experience was proof she had truly come to terms with her past. Something she didn't realize she cared so much about until now.

He looked at her in silence before he nodded. "You appear a little obsessed with your personal space. I'm wondering how you're going to handle our dance lessons."

How did she answer that? Lexi was the only one who knew about her issues and that wasn't going to change. She'd dealt with it for years without any problems, mostly because of a good therapist. She'd deal with the dancing thing when the time came. Really, the fact she didn't get all worked up when he touched her was a good thing. And took away some of the anxiety about the lessons.

"It's just one of my quirks. It's not going to be a problem for dancing, so no need to worry. Right now, I'm mentally exhausted, and I want a little extra space. Is it really such a big deal?"

"Do you want me to go first or bring up the rear?"

Rear? The last thing she needed was to watch *that* all the way to the ground floor. "I'll go first."

He swept out a hand in front of him. "After you."

She sucked in a deep breath before she stepped past him and continued down. Which she realized was a mistake when her nostrils filled with his scent. She was several steps ahead before he started to follow. It didn't take her long to realize this set up wasn't any better. Yeah, she had her personal space and then some, but she'd swear his gaze burned into her as they descended. When she reached the landing and turned towards him to head down the next flight, she caught him in the act.

She raised her brows. "Getting an eyeful?"

He smiled slightly. "Not yet. Maybe by the time we reach the bottom. Your legs are mesmerizing."

"You're such a gentleman. I'm flattered."

"I do my best." He paused. "Seriously, though, Jade, I'd like to know why you became an accountant."

She bit back a sigh of resignation. There were worse things to talk about. He was going to be part of her life so a desire to get to know her better was normal. As was her physical reaction to him. *Normal.*

"I started working for some family friends who had their own firm when I was in high school. I liked it enough to become certified myself and when they passed away, they left me the business as well as the building it was in. It has an apartment on the second floor which I was renting from them at the time, and I still live there. Not so impressive anymore, is it?"

"Mmmm…"

That vibrated through her, and she tried to control a shiver.

"Maybe not as impressive as building it up on your own, but you must be good to have kept the business going. How long has that been?"

"Seven years."

"See?"

She lifted a shoulder. "Whatever. Your turn. Where are you from, and how did you end up in America?"

"I don't know…That's two questions."

She looked over her shoulder and wrinkled her nose at him. "You are *so* annoying."

"*Gracias.* No one's ever called me that before. Slave driver, sadist, perfectionist, yes. But annoying? No."

"You save that charming side of yourself for me, then?" She turned to head down the next flight of stairs and caught his huge grin.

"*Si.* Only for you, *chica.*"

"Thanks." Her stomach did a flip, and she was annoyed with herself for feeling like it was a *good* thing. It was the smile. It had to be the smile.

"Well, Ms. Uptight…"

And the voice. That moniker shouldn't seem like an endearment.

"Since you asked so nicely, I'll answer both your questions. I was born and raised in San Juan, Puerto Rico and my—er, what is the word? Mentor, sent me to America to go to school at UCLA."

She whistled softly, and it echoed around the stairwell. "You had to be an impressive dancer to have a mentor spend that kind of money on you." As she turned to head down the next flight, she caught him scowling. She looked down at her feet as she continued, "You're one hell of a sexy guy. Did you have a sugar mama?" She bit her lip and cursed herself before quickly trying to fix what she'd done. "Oh brother. I am a mess right now. That remark was uncalled for."

"*Ai ai ai!* I do not know this *sugar mama*, but I can guess, and *hell no!* What do you take me for?"

She shook her head and tried to appear careless by shrugging. "Really, I'm sorry, but in my defense, it's California and that stuff happens here." Anxious to get off the subject she asked, "Is UCLA where you met Beck?"

He didn't answer, and for a few long, drawn-out moments, the only noise was the hollow echo of their footsteps. She'd stepped over a line, and he had every right to be mad. She deserved whatever he dished out but was flooded with relief when he merely answered her question.

"It is. We shared a dorm room our first year and ended up making a great team. He helped me with my English classes; I helped him with math."

"I wouldn't expect an artistic type like you to have math skills." She bit her tongue. What was it about him that made her brain turn off and smart remarks fly out of her mouth before she knew what was happening? Had she been transported to some sort of parallel universe? Where was poised, methodical, *uptight* Jade?

"I'm starting to get the impression you *enjoy* bickering with me."

"Hmmm...Maybe I do, though God knows I shouldn't. It does give me a bit of a thrill." Along with other things there was no way she'd admit to him. "Generally I keep that stuff to myself, but there's something special about you that has me saying things I shouldn't." She smiled over her shoulder at him and he gave her a quick half-smile.

"Ah, c*hica,* I give women all kinds of thrills." He chuckled. "Although, now you know two of my well-kept secrets, I must be careful about ticking you off."

"You are *such* a celebrity."

"Ah, ah, ah…Watch it. I know how to keep you in line."

He ran a finger down her arm. How did he get so close without her realizing it? Her personal space alarm didn't go off. She suppressed a shiver of delight, fought the urge to get closer and picked up her pace. No doubt he was used to females falling at his feet in adoration, and she was determined not to be one. "So, what's your degree?"

"Bachelor of Arts with a minor in business. Yours?"

She tossed her head. "An associate's degree in accounting." She blew out a breath. Why did she feel so defensive about that? Until now she'd been darn proud. He cleared his throat but didn't say anything and to relieve the awkwardness, as though she needed to defend her lack of a full college degree, she blurted, "My mom died my senior year of high school and it was up to me to take care of Lexi. My stepfather…" Her turn to clear her throat. Before she realized it had happened, she was on a subject she avoided like the plague. "Well, shall we say, we were better off without him."

"I lost my mother when I was five."

She looked over her shoulder at him and was surprised at the expressionless look on his face. "That's tough."

"I suppose."

As she struggled with what to say, the stairwell door flew open and knocked her sideways into the cement wall. She hit her shoulder and head so hard it had her slithering to the floor, and the man that barreled through it would've knocked Han over and down the stairs if he hadn't grabbed the railing and jumped back out of the way so quickly. The guy's "Sorry, dude!" as he flew down the stairs and out of sight lacked sincerity.

"Jerk!" She yelled after him, her voice echoing around the stairwell as she turned to Han. "You are impressively quick. Are you all right? Did that guy hurt you?"

He sat on the opposite side of the stairway rather green around the gills and sweat beaded his upper lip. A wave of dizziness washed over her, and she had to fight the need to toss her cookies. Gingerly she touched the side of her head and sucked in her breath on a hiss. She had a good-sized bump, and when she looked at her hand, it was smeared with blood. *Well, isn't that just the icing on the cake?*

Han swore profusely in Spanish. Quite a number of words she'd never heard before and had no desire to learn. "*Chica*, you are bleeding."

He moved to sit next to her, and she ignored him as she dug around in her purse for something she could use to keep the blood from dripping down her face and found a nearly empty packet of tissues. *About time something went right.* Before she could pull one out, he took the packet, extracted one and applied it tenderly to her injury.

"What is it with people?" He removed the tissue and dabbed at the side of her face to wipe away the blood. "It doesn't seem to be bleeding too badly, *gracias a Dios.*"

"Don't worry, I'm fine," she lied, not sure which

made her more dizzy, the bump on her head or his nearness. She struggled to ignore the warm, squishy feeling she got from his genuine concern and the gentle way he was caring for her injury. It was so unexpected from someone like him.

He raised his brows. "An accountant *and* a doctor."

She attempted a smile.

"You have a pretty good-sized lump here, and I don't like it. Are you hurt anywhere else?"

"My shoulder will probably have a bruise, but everything else seems fine. I hit the wall pretty hard but didn't fall down or anything."

He placed the tissue on her injury again, then dabbed at it a couple times before he crumpled it in his hand and shoved it, as well as the packet, into his pants pocket. He took a quick look over his shoulder.

"We're on the ninth floor; are you going to be able to make it the rest of the way down?"

"Yes. I'm okay. Really. Head wounds tend to be bloody but aren't as bad as they seem. I just want to get home and start over again tomorrow. Thankfully it's Saturday, so I can lounge around and recover from any lingering effects."

She awkwardly hauled herself to her feet, then gasped as she swayed. She better not have a concussion because she was in no mood for more complications.

Han wrapped an arm around her waist to keep her from falling. "Maybe we better wait a bit. I do not need you passing out and falling down the stairs."

She moved out of his hold. "I'm fine. Just stood too quickly."

"You're an interesting shade of gray…"

"I'm *fine*. Let's get out of here. I am *over* this

whole evening."

****

His wrist throbbed unmercifully, and he felt slightly nauseous, but what bothered him more was the sensations this woman had bubbling to the surface. Seeing her crumpled up on the stairs gave him a strange feeling in his gut, and when she pulled her hand away from her head and there was blood on it, the feeling spread through his body. He had an overwhelming urge to do whatever was humanly possible to make sure she was okay. He didn't dare think about why. It was foreign. It was weird. And though he didn't like it, he couldn't ignore it. The only thing he was capable of ignoring was his own injury so he could care for her.

And what was the deal with that? His body was his livelihood, his temple. He had it insured, for goodness' sake. He should be having a meltdown about his arm being out of commission, but instead, he barely felt the pain. It was over-shadowed by what his stomach did when he saw blood oozing out of Jade's head, changing her hair to red. He feared if it was any worse, he would be useless.

Damn it! It wasn't even his first time around an injured woman. It was part of the territory in his line of work, and it never affected him like this. He felt bad about it, did what he could to fix things and moved on. The show must go on.

He pulled the tissue packet out of his pocket, extracted the last one, and wiped away the fresh blood. "It looks like the bleeding has slowed down."

"Good. I'm fine. Really."

"Well, I'm taking you to a doctor anyway." He braced himself.

She groaned and compressed her lips. "I don't need a doctor. I need to go home."

"I know exactly how you feel." He paused. "Do you live alone?" A reasonable question, but his muscles tensed anyway.

"Yes. Like it's any of your business."

At least she was behaving normally. For her, anyway. His shoulders relaxed. And it had nothing to do with the fact she didn't have a live-in boyfriend. *It didn't*.

"I'm not sending you home by yourself when you may have a concussion. I want a doctor's verdict. End of discussion. But first we have to get down the rest of the stairs. Keep the tissue pressed to your wound to help stop the bleeding."

She gave him an exasperated look as she did as she was told and started down. Her hand was gripping the railing so tight her knuckles were white, but other than that she seemed all right.

He wanted to pick her up and carry her to his car, which had him grinding his teeth for a number of reasons, least of which was the injury to his wrist that made it impossible. He'd like to put his arm around her for support but was worried how she'd react to the invasion of her personal space. The purpose was to alleviate her problems—not add to them. He scowled. She wasn't the only one living on the edge right now. At least they were almost to the ground floor.

When the valet pulled up to the front of the hotel with his Porsche, she surprised him again.

"Oh my God, *this* is your car? I've always wanted to own a Porsche convertible. It's a fantasy come true to ride in one."

She quickly walked over to it and ran her hands lovingly, *caressingly*, along its curves and lines as she circled the car. Only one thought pounded through his brain as he watched her. He wanted those hands running over him. And did she have to say *fantasy*? He was having one of his own right now, and it revolved around the hood of the car.

He stifled a groan as she stopped and stood there with her legs slightly apart, hands caressing the fender, her pale hair a glittering waterfall down her back. *Did she have any idea what she looked like?* When he forced himself to look elsewhere, he noticed he wasn't the only one caught up in the picture she made. The valets were drooling.

"Okay. Enough paying homage to my car. Get in. Emergency Room, remember?" It was more an effort to remind himself than anything. He was throbbing all over.

"Yeah, right. Sorry. Any chance I can drive?"

"Nope. Keep that in fantasy land."

He walked around the hood of the car as she got in. He wasn't sure he could handle looking at those legs as she climbed in the car. He didn't trust himself. His hand braced on the open car door, he looked across the roof and silently cursed himself. He'd given the valets something else to lust over. He should've opened the door for her and blocked their view. He could've touched her then too and had a good reason for it.

Wait a minute. Since when had it bothered him to have other men salivating over the woman he was with? It happened all the time, and he enjoyed the envy.

He shook his head as he climbed behind the wheel, his injury painfully reminding him he had a bigger problem. He had to drive a stick-shift with his wrist trashed from his maneuver in the stairwell. Still, better an arm than a leg. So, since he had a lifetime of experience pushing past the pain, he sucked it up and headed towards Cedars Sinai, his hospital of choice, and thankfully close by.

****

Now what?

Han was passed out in the passenger seat and she needed to get him inside. At least he'd programmed the GPS before he conked out, so she found his house without his help. *She* was the one to drive *him* home. Not that she hadn't thoroughly enjoyed driving his car. That made everything worth it. Well, maybe…She blew out an exasperated breath. This nightmare wasn't anywhere close to over. He'd made such a big deal over her when he was the one seriously injured. She was sore and had a bit of a headache, but bumps and bruises were all she had to deal with. She didn't need stitches, much less have the concussion he was worried about.

Han, on the other hand, injured his wrist when he grabbed the railing and twisted out of the way to keep from getting knocked down the stairs. Now he was sporting an air cast and drugged up on pain meds.

She shook him vigorously by the shoulder; thankfully it roused him. "Han. We're at your house. I'm thinking you should've waited until you got home to take the pain killers."

"Hmmm?"

She shook him again. "*Wake up.* We have to go inside, and not only can I not carry you, I can't get inside either."

He swiped a hand down his face and sat up in the

seat. "*Sí*. We're here already?"

She suppressed a sarcastic remark. "Yep."

He fumbled with his seatbelt but appeared to be coming out of his lethargy. "Um, how about pulling in the garage?"

She gave him an exasperated look. It was some ugly hour of the morning; she was beyond tired. "I don't have the code, *genius,* and I see no garage door opener in here."

"Oh yeah...Right." He shook his head in an attempt to clear it. She doubted it did anything. "Garage door opener." He pushed a hidden button and a compartment opened to reveal the opener. He hit the button of the remote and the door made its slow climb up. After she pulled inside, he pushed the control button again, and the door closed. She shut off the car and looked over at him. He was staring blankly out the windshield. The timed light of the door opener shut off. Brilliant. Now they were sitting in a dark garage.

"We still need to get inside the house."

"Give me a minute. I'm getting there. Why don't you open the car door? It should give you enough light to find the light switch. It's by the door to the house."

"Yeah, wouldn't have figured that out on my own," she muttered as she shoved the door open. She sighed. She was tired and crabby, but that was no reason to be nasty.

When his pain killers kicked in and he realized he shouldn't drive, they decided she'd spend what was left of the night at his house. By the time they were inside and he was safely in his king-sized bed, she was completely exhausted. So incredibly tired she saw no problem taking one of his t-shirts and a pair of sweat pants and changing into them so she could sleep comfortably. She was beyond over wearing a dress.

After changing in his *en suite* bathroom, she crept across his bedroom and headed to the door. When a wave of mental and emotional exhaustion washed over her, she sat down on the opposite side of the bed from Han, scrubbed her hands down her face and smothered a huge yawn. What she wouldn't give to be able to lie down right here instead of wander around a strange house trying to find a place to sleep. For a moment she wished she hadn't agreed to this plan; then she decided it was better than having him spend the night at her house. She just needed a moment to regroup before she went wandering around in search of a bedroom. If there even was another one. She groaned softly and yawned again. If not, she'd have to hunt up a blanket and crash on the couch.

Just thinking about walking made her want to collapse where she was. It was one more thing she'd have to do before she could sleep. Too bad he didn't give her a little more info before the drugs kicked in. Was her head ever pounding. Maybe she should've taken the pain killers the hospital offered, but the accountant in her wouldn't let her pay the outrageous fee they'd charge.

A movement in the corner of her eye caught her attention, and she turned toward the head of the bed. The dim bedside lamp illuminated the room enough she could see a sleek black cat reclining there, staring at her with eyes she swore were the same color as Han's. Its tail twitched slowly back and forth as he decided whether or not to pounce. How had she missed seeing that beautiful creature before? Was she dreaming with her eyes open? She swiped a hand down her face. Nope, still there. And she was not up for being pounced on and mauled by a cat in her sleep. Though it would be no surprise if that was how this hideous night ended.

Slowly she laid down on her side and rested her head on the pillow to show the cat she wasn't a threat. Then she reached out a hand and let him sniff her fingers, which he did with a touch of disdain. She smiled, then stifled a yawn. Typical. The tail twitching slowed, so she ran the back of her finger from his forehead over the top of his head and down his neck. He butted his head against it, the tail stopped twitching and the purring started.

"Aren't you beautiful?" she whispered. "I wonder what your name is?" No collar with a name tag, so he was an indoor cat. "Are we going to be friends? You make me miss having a kitty."

He stood, stretched, circled around and planted himself next to her, leaning back against her chest. She stroked him from head to tail, and the purring increased. She hadn't owned a cat since she was ten, but as this one cuddled up against her, she had the desire to have one again. She caressed him behind the ears, then rhythmically stroked his back. She should look into getting a cat. It would be nice to have a little company around the house. What were the odds Han would let her have this one?

****

He was in her bed again. Where was Lexi? Why hadn't she slept with Lexi? She kicked her legs and swung her arms in an effort to make him leave her alone.

"No, no. Please, I don't want this."

But he didn't listen. He never listened. He just kept *touching*…and his hands were everywhere at once. Those horrible, rough, incredibly strong hands that she couldn't get away from no matter what she did. She struggled anyway and pushed at them, desperate to get them *off*. If she didn't get them off her, she'd go crazy. She was halfway there as it was, maniacally obsessed with the need to be free of those awful hands.

Jade's eyes flew open with a gasp. Nothing was familiar, and a male hand rested on her stomach. It was happening again. She screamed, rolled away, and landed on the floor in a heap, all tangled up in the bedding. She screamed again and flailed her legs wildly in an effort to untangle herself from the bedspread.

She finally managed to kick herself free and as she rolled away from the bed, her escape was blocked by two bare masculine legs. She was trapped between the legs and the bed.

With a whimper she surrendered, squeezed her eyes shut, and went completely still. She feared any movement on her part would make things worse. At least she had herself under control enough to do that.

"Are you all right?"

That voice. That bone-melting accent. She blew out a breath. Two tears seeped out from under her lids and trickled down to her ears. Her locket. Where was her locket? Her fingers fumbled around her neck until she located the chain and pulled it out from under her shirt. She traced the chain until her fingers reached the locket at the end and held on for dear life. The adrenaline rush receded and left her weak and shaky. *Guess they were even now*.

She didn't say anything; she couldn't, so she jerked

her head in a nod. It took all she had to keep the shiver creeping up her spine from visibly manifesting itself and humiliating her even more. Besides, she didn't think she could handle seeing *Alejandro Rivera* in his boxers first thing in the morning. It had been enough of an eyeful last night in dim lighting. With a scruff in the full light of day? More than she could deal with at the moment. She tightened her hand around the locket until it dug painfully into her palm, grounding her in the present.

He didn't move away. She sensed his presence and the silence dragged on. She was *not* opening her eyes yet—maybe when her heart started beating at a more normal rate.

"Just wondering…Are you planning on spending the whole day down there?"

He chuckled, and she appreciated his attempt to lighten the atmosphere.

"Shut up."

She laid a forearm over her eyes. *Deep calming breaths. Just keep breathing slowly and deeply. You'll be okay in a bit.* She shot to her feet. He leaped back; she smothered a smile. *Damn* was he ever graceful…And so hot she thought she'd melt. She suppressed a shiver. Talk about doing a one-eighty. She just woke from a nightmare she hadn't had in years, one that normally left her even more determined to avoid men, but here she was admiring one.

He put his hands on his hips. "Well, that's certainly an interesting way to wake up. Are you okay?"

She brushed her tangled hair off her face and nodded her head. In an effort to appear careless, she shrugged a shoulder. "Nightmare."

"No kidding. You're okay now, though?"

"Yes, but I'd rather not talk about it. How's the wrist?"

Now he shrugged. "Sore."

She bit back her own *No kidding*. "You were too out of it last night to tell me what the doctor said."

"I've pulled some ligaments so it'll be useless for a while, but nothing that will keep me from working at my dance studio. Some state-of-the-art treatments, as well as some not-so-state-of-the-art icing, and I'll be as good as new."

"That's a relief." In an effort to avoid silence, she asked, "So, when you say, 'my dance studio' do you mean *yours* or where you work?"

He ran his fingers through his hair and blew out a breath. "Mine. I bought it a few months back. I'm retiring from professional dancing and going in a more business-oriented direction. You're looking at the new owner of Seriously Dance."

"Wow. You don't seem old enough to retire." She smiled and gave him the once over with the intent to look for evidence of aging. *Big mistake.* Her heart rate sped up, and it had nothing to do with her nightmare. All that bronzed skin on display and a muscular chest covered with just enough dark hair to make her hands itch to see what it felt like. The novelty of being in such close proximity with a mostly naked man who was no threat held her enthralled. In an effort to keep her hands to herself, as well as prevent her mind from spiraling into her past, she reached for her locket and rubbed it between forefinger and thumb.

He rolled his eyes, a faint smile tugging at his lips. "Sometimes people retire because they can, not because they're old. Now, as exciting as this conversation is, I'd prefer to be having it in my clothes. Do you mind?" He raised his brows. "And you're welcome, by the way."

"What for?"

"The clothes you borrowed last night."

"Consider it repayment for hauling you home," she said over one shoulder as she left the room—and closed the door before he could reply.

It didn't drown out his question. "What's for breakfast? I'd love something hot, and I can't do it on my own. My wrist, remember?"

Simply because he'd hassled her about using his clothes, she decided to leave them on while she rounded up something to eat. Sure, he was annoying and yeah, she'd already gone above and beyond, but still. It was Alejandro Rivera for crying out loud. She was living every woman's fantasy. How many women would kill to be in her shoes right now? So, she'd help him out by fixing him—*them*—a hot breakfast.

Never mind this once-in-a-lifetime opportunity to spend the morning in a Malibu beach house. The open-plan living room featured an entire wall of windows with a view of the ocean. To be able to step out the back door onto the beach fell into the realm of fantasy come true. Everything about this guy fulfilled one fantasy or another. *Not going there...*

Focus on the kitchen. That's a fantasy, too. Ultra-modern, stainless steel appliances, dark cupboards with brushed silver hardware, and a mosaic tile backsplash in reds, grays, black and white. Cooking in there would be a treat and watching the ocean while she did it...She let out a sigh of delight. The troubles she experienced yesterday might very well be worth the tradeoff.

She'd just turned off the burners on the scrambled eggs, bacon, and hash browns and was searching for plates when he wandered into the kitchen and propped a hip on the end of the breakfast bar.

"*Angelito mío,* my stomach and my wrist thank you."

When he grinned, his eyes sparkled like champagne, and left her feeling like she'd downed a whole bottle of the stuff. By sheer effort of will she looked away and tried to remember what she was doing. *Plates.* She needed plates for the food. And cups for the coffee. Most importantly, she needed coffee.

"Are you being nosy, or do you need something?"

That was more like it. She regained some of her equilibrium. "I don't know…Do you usually eat your food out of the pan it was cooked in?"

He nodded his head towards her. "You're almost there. Next cupboard over."

She pulled out what they needed, loaded their plates and after getting out the silverware, which she found in an earlier search, she set the plates on the breakfast bar, careful not to look at him again—or get too close. Apparently the crazy sensations he aroused last night weren't a one-off. She desperately needed some coffee and food to give her the strength not to do something stupid. Like kiss him again. She felt the color rush to her cheeks and turned away from him so he couldn't guess what she was thinking.

She sneaked a glance at him to find he was watching her, and it took all her concentration not to fumble around and make a mess of things. She bit the inside of her cheek rather hard as she tried to pour coffee in their cups without sloshing it all over the ubermodern cement counter top. And was rather proud of herself for actually doing it. However, she had to take a bracing sip of the brew before setting his next to his plate. All the while making a concerted effort not to look at him.

"I'm going to need your help."

What? Surely he could eat with one hand. No way she was feeding him breakfast. "Not happening. You can feed yourself."

"Not eating, *chica*, though now you mention it…"

Not looking. Not looking. *Not looking.* She was having a hard enough time coping with imagining the look on his face, the expression in his eyes. She stifled a groan at the thought. Was he seriously attracted to her? Or was he just doing his Devil-of-the-Dance-Floor routine? She was nothing special, just ordinary Jade Nichols, who garnered some attention from the male species, but none of them the caliber of Alejandro Rivera. He didn't seem the type to have a macho need to conquer every woman he encountered, so what was the deal?

She stiffened her spine. She wasn't looking for a romantic relationship, and if she was, it certainly wouldn't be with a celebrity. Add in the fact, as Beck's best friend, they were going to be around each other for years to come, so getting involved as anything more than friends was a very bad idea. First step in doing that was to keep her distance and do her best to maintain the uptight impression she'd given him last night. Or most of last night, anyway. Seriously, there was no reason for her to be so worked up over him. He was just a *man.* Like half the population on the planet. She turned toward him.

"You can remove *that* thought and tell me what it is you really need."

"Help getting this back on." He held up his air cast and elastic bandage. "I took it off for my shower and am having a hard time putting it back on."

Getting close to him.

Panic welled as a flashback of the nightmare returned. Her body went rigid. She took a deep breath and let it out slowly as she ran a finger over her locket. This was not her stepfather. But…Had all that up-close-and-personal with him last night been the catalyst to the old nightmare returning after years of hibernation? The thoughts and feelings his nearness aroused were scary in a different way. Would her life ever be the same once Lexi's wedding was over?

"Wrapping your wrist. Really?" She swiped a hand down her face and blew out an exasperated breath. "Sorry. Still trying to recover from last night. And waiting for the coffee to kick in."

"Not much of a morning person, are you?" His gaze wandered over her face. The look in his eyes made it hard to discern what he was thinking. He tipped his head back to look at the ceiling for a moment then put the bandage and cast on the counter and started towards her. Her breath hitched in her chest, but he merely moved past her, headed to the refrigerator. Opening the freezer door, he dug around inside.

"I just remembered I should probably ice it first, so let's eat while I do that." Pulling out an ice pack, he held it on his arm as he went to the breakfast bar to sit.

Rather than take the seat next to him, she pulled her plate across the counter so she could stand opposite him while she ate. She was pretty sure she wouldn't be able to get anything down if she sat next to him. She needed to psyche herself up for bandaging his arm. She went a little lightheaded at the thought of touching him and brushed a finger over her locket again. It was a testament to how tense she was when the cat rubbed against her leg and she had to stifle a scream. She looked down at it and wrinkled her nose.

"Your cat is the reason I ended up in your bed rather than somewhere else. Fell asleep making friends with it."

He gave her a half smile, took a sip of coffee then told the cat, "Well, well, well, Flamenco, it's come to that now? I need your help to get a woman in my bed?"

****

This had to be one of the stupidest ideas he'd come up with lately. It would've been painful and sloppy, but he could've strapped his arm up on his own. He'd wanted an excuse to be near her again. Why?

Why in the world would he want to get any more entangled than he had to with a woman who not only wasn't his type, but had issues? Giving dance lessons to a person who didn't want him touching her wasn't bad enough? He had to look for reasons to get close to her? And what *was* it about her that made him feel and act so out of character? She had that stupid dress on again and her hair was pulled back in the clip.

"This really looks painful, Han. It's so swollen. I'm worried I'll hurt you while I'm wrapping it."

"It hurts; I won't deny it. But I've had worse *and* had to dance through it. Just wrap it back up the best you can. And do me a favor. When you get home, burn that dress."

Her eyes flew to his face. "What? Why? There's

nothing wrong with this dress. It's in good shape. I hardly ever wear it."

"Thank God. Seriously. Part of my job is knowing something about clothes. And that dress isn't—suited for you. It doesn't do you justice. Get rid of it and find something more flattering. You'd be a knock out in the right dress. Especially with those stilettos."

"I don't even know what to say to that. But you might want to shut up so I can concentrate on your arm. I don't want to hurt you unnecessarily."

Probably in his best interests to take that advice. So he did. She shifted his arm to make it easier for her to wrap the bandage and he winced. Then she bent forward some more, and suddenly it was all worth it. The view rivaled the one out his windows. Maybe it was the vantage point, but suddenly, she had a figure. She was skinny, much skinnier than he liked, but that didn't mean she didn't have curves where it counted. It was the clothes that kept him from realizing it. The unflattering dress, his T-shirt and sweatpants. One look and his imagination went wild. Probably not a good thing for him or for her. She was wound up so tight he didn't dare say anything, much less touch her in any way. Her nightmare gave him some insight and took the thrill out of pushing her buttons in that regard.

"As soon as you're done with this, I'll take you home. Where do you live?"

"Santa Monica. You didn't take any more of those painkillers, did you?"

He snorted. "I'm not stupid. I'm only taking those at night so I can sleep. Ibuprofen is enough to take the edge off during the day." He clenched his jaw when an unexpected stab of pain went up his arm. "We can program your address into the GPS, and you can sit back and enjoy the ride along the Pacific Coast Highway."

Her head jerked once in acknowledgment, and her eyes darted sideways. Maybe he wasn't the only one reeling from their latest up close and personal. "That would be nice. I haven't done it in a while."

He sighed. *Beck, you better appreciate the sacrifice I'm making to give you this wedding gift.*

Chapter Five

It felt *so* good to finally close her front door behind her. With a gusty sigh she leaned against it, then mentally cursed her sister. Two months of that man in her life? After less than twenty-four hours, she was physically and emotionally exhausted. And her desire for him to kiss her again made her even more angry. At herself.

He had the gall to suggest she burn her black dress. She ground her teeth when she thought of something else to add to his list of sins. She'd given him a great view down the front of her dress. Now he knew she liked frivolous underwear. Even worse, why did remembering the look in his eyes when he blatantly stared down her dress make her want to strip for him? If this was what she'd missed by avoiding men, then she wasn't missing much. She squeezed her eyes shut and all the sensations of that kiss in the elevator flooded her, almost as intensely as when it happened. Maybe she *was* missing out on something great.

She pushed herself away from the door, hung her purse on the coat rack and headed down the hall, unzipping her dress as she went and shimmying out of it when she reached the bedroom. *He* hadn't liked it, but was it really that bad? It was just a black dress for crying out loud…Viciously she kicked at it, sending it flying across the hardwood floor to disappear under the bed. Why did she even care what he thought? She removed her black stilettos, walked over to the closet, and placed them neatly back in their box.

If circumstances hadn't forced them together, he never would've looked twice at her, and she better remember that. She discarded her underwear and put it in the dirty-clothes basket, pulled out some fresh ones, randomly grabbed a t-shirt and yoga pants and headed to the bathroom. She was not uptight. She was not prim and proper. She was not anal. She was standing here naked, wasn't she? She stopped in the doorway, sighed in defeat and leaned a shoulder against the jam. Okay, maybe she was. But not being able to leave her dress in a heap under the bed was a *good* thing. What was wrong with cleaning up after yourself and making sure everything was done right the first time? Having your shoes organized was a good thing too.

Turning around, she went over to the bed, set her clothes down on it, and retrieved the dress. She shook it out in front of her. Damn him...*Damn him!* It *was* hideous.

Even if it wasn't, because of him she'd never wear it again. Balling it up, she threw it in the trash. It was time for a new one anyway. She needed something for the rehearsal dinner; she could use it for her standby, need-to-wear-something-dressy type dress. Which was rarely for her, so no big deal.

Now, a shower, then maybe she'd do some number puzzles. She was not going to watch that recording on her DVR of the dance competition program, *Celebrity Dance*, starring Alejandro Rivera. She'd be deleting that. Maybe...*Maybe?* Definitely!

After she watched it one more time. She heaved a

sigh in defeat.

****

It was pretty bad when a number puzzle didn't clear her head. She threw her pen down on the table in disgust and propped her head on her hands. If this was her state after spending time with Alejandro Rivera, what would she be like after a dance lesson? She shuddered. But oh, the thought of letting her sister down on her wedding day…That was worth a shudder, too.

Lexi. She'd left early last night due to a migraine. Until now, it hadn't occurred to Jade to call and make sure she was okay. If she didn't get her medication soon enough, she would be in bad shape and might need help. She picked up her cell phone.

"Hey, kid, how you doing?"

"Much better. Beck took great care of me; I got my medicine in time and can cope with life today. Sorry I abandoned you to Han last night. I hope it wasn't too awkward."

Awkward didn't come close. And though she longed to talk to someone about the emotional roller coaster ride she'd been on during the last twelve hours, she wasn't about to burden her sister. She didn't want to mess up the wedding plans. Plus, worrying about if she and Han were getting along was something Lexi didn't need to be doing. Still, there was a pause that lasted a bit too long as she figured out what to say.

"It was fine. The dessert you ordered was heavenly and well worth being alone with Han. Besides, his car is to die for."

Lexi laughed, a sound Jade was always happy to hear because it meant she was doing things right. "I thought that might make up for things. As if Han isn't enough for you to drool over, though I bet you got more of a thrill from his car than from him. You're just that crazy."

Jade laughed, hoping it didn't come across as strained as it felt. The thrill Han gave her was so far beyond the excitement of driving her dream car. "Well, now I know saving every last penny to get one is worth the sacrifice. But back to you. You're sure you're okay? You don't need me to get anything for you? My day is blessedly free and clear, so I'm available if you need something. I could come by and give you my top-notch, migraine-relieving massage."

The silence that came at the question was rather unnerving. Was something wrong that Lexi didn't want her to know about? Was she sicker than she'd let on? Or had she lied about the headache?

"Jade, please don't take this the wrong way, I love you to bits and am so thankful I had you to take care of me when Mom died. And your massages really are top notch. But you don't need to worry about me so much. I have Beck for that now. Besides, it's time you focused on you now and indulged yourself instead of me."

Pain arced through her heart at the thought Lexi didn't need her anymore. It was bound to happen at some point, she just hadn't thought about *when* it happened. It suddenly felt as though she'd lost her purpose in life. Which was absolutely stupid. Her world didn't revolve around Lexi any more than Lexi's revolved around her. Still, it was hard to think of her sister as an adult who could take care of herself, even though she'd been one for years. She swallowed a lump in her throat and blinked away tears. Why wasn't she better prepared for this step? Had she buried her head in the sand because she didn't want to think about a future without Lexi to care for?

"I know. You're right. Old habits are hard to break, you know? I'm glad you're feeling better."

"Thanks, Jay-Jay," she said softly, then cleared her throat. "With all the drama last night, I forgot to tell you your dress is in. I have to call them on Monday to set up fittings for both of us. I need to know what works for you."

"I'll have a look at my schedule and text you what works. I can let you know by tomorrow night. Is that okay?"

"Sounds good. Love you more than chocolate and kitties."

"Love you more than number puzzles and cheesecake. Talk to you soon."

The text alert on her phone went off immediately after she ended the call with Lexi. She jumped at the unexpected noise and looked at the message—and fought the urge to throw the phone on the table. How did he get her cell number? *Lexi*. It had to be.

*Chica need ur help with my business accounts. B there in 1 hour.Sí? *

Squeezing her eyes shut, she pinched the bridge of her nose and blew out a frustrated breath. Like he would really listen to her if she told her 'no'. What were the odds looking at his books would get her mind away from the man who owned them? It depended on where he was when she did it. What were the odds he would give the info to her and leave? Slim to none, probably, considering the way things were going for her lately. Still…Maybe confronting her demons would help her move on, and at the moment, he was one of her biggest ones.

She responded: *OMG. R u stalking me?*

LOL! No. I m humiliating myself in front of u again. So?

C u soon.

Right after she hit send, she realized she had absolutely no desire to confront her demons. She wanted to run screaming away from them. The thought of taking dance lessons made her stomach churn. And the fact Han was a celebrity had nothing to do with it. They were going to be up close and personal for a lot longer than when they'd kissed.

Would she enjoy it, or would it be too much?

Would it bring up all those feelings she'd worked hard to overcome? Still, she was excited at the thought of seeing him again. Oddly enough the desire to primp jumped into the mix. Even though she had no idea where to start. She hadn't primped for a guy since high school; even then, it hadn't been something she developed a knack for.

Not happening, Jade.

A T-shirt and yoga pants were what she'd be wearing for her dance lessons. He might as well see her like that now. And the French braid, too. It was comfortable and kept her hair out of her face. Perfect for work, perfect for dancing. Problem solved.

So what the hell was she supposed to do until he got here? She had difficulty concentrating before the text came in. No way she could manage it now.

Cheesecake. It would keep her hands and head busy. There was enough time for it, and when she was done doing whatever it was he needed her to, it would be cooled and ready to enjoy.

****

Not an excuse. Not. An. Excuse.

Han figured if he told himself that often enough, it would be true. And it *was*. Mostly. He knew something wasn't right with the books for Let's Dance, his dance studio for under-privileged children. The studio came as part of the deal when he bought Seriously Dance and was the chief motivator for the purchase. His math skills were definitely rusty, but had he the desire, he knew he could decipher the problem. It bothered him that he couldn't easily figure it out. He was smarter than that.

Face it, Rivera; it's an excuse.

He hated that his gut churned with excitement at the thought of seeing Jade again. Being with a woman, whether working or relaxing, was always fun but never—He absolutely refused to use the word emotional. He didn't do emotion. His childhood cured him of that. And if it hadn't, Marguerite's death certainly would have.

By the time he pulled up at her house—for the second time that day—he was thoroughly disgusted with himself. He growled, threw open the car door, giving it a good slam once he climbed out, and headed up the stairs to her apartment. Two sharp raps on her door that were probably harder than they needed to be, and there she was.

Tall and skinny, taller than he usually felt comfortable with, but she had a figure all right and it was amazing. As was the smell that wafted out the door. *Cheesecake*...From that day forward, a smell that would have him thinking about things that had nothing to do with cheesecake. Now it was one with the hottest body he'd ever seen. He clenched his jaw. Since when had yoga pants and a tight, wash-worn t-shirt with a math equation on it he was too fuddled to decipher become sexy? When they showed off a tiny waist which highlighted a chest his hands itched to caress, that's when. *Hell...*

He cleared a suddenly tight throat and gave his head a slight shake. "I wanted to go straight to the dance studio; everything's on the computer there, but suddenly I'm feeling the need for a piece of cheesecake."

She grabbed her purse from a hook by the door and told him, "Get over it. It's too hot to eat right now."

"My taste buds are saying they don't care, but I know it will be much better for the wait." No double entendre there...At this point he felt desperate enough to slam his injured wrist against something hard to take his mind off her. "So what are you waiting for? Let's go."

She gave him an exasperated look and the light bulb came on. Too close. He, on the other hand, was fighting the overwhelming desire to get closer. *Cheesecake, Han, all the better for the wait.* He stepped back and swept his hand out. "After you, *chica.*"

****

She was *way* too white for this part of town and though safely ensconced in Han's office, scrolling through his accounts on the computer, she was glad he was there with her. Actually, she was amazed she could comprehend anything with him hanging over her shoulder, his breath warm on her neck—something she was loathe to admit she enjoyed.

He was right. Something was definitely hinky here. The building needed some serious repairs—at the very least Han's office could use a serious cleaning, much less furniture that wasn't thirty years old—yet according to the books, there wasn't a cash flow problem. Granted, fund raising had been neglected since Han took over and cash was running low, but still…

She squeezed her eyes shut, pinched the bridge of her nose and ground her teeth. He smelled as good today as he had in the elevator. As comforting as his presence was, she couldn't get a handle on his books while he hovered. She dropped her hand and opened her eyes.

"What? Did you find something already?"

"No. You're going to have to back off. My brain shuts down when someone gets too close."

She clamped her mouth shut before anything too revealing fell out of it. He knew she liked a big personal space bubble, so he shouldn't question her request. Hoping it would distract him from her revelation, she continued talking. "Though I *can* tell something's not right."

"What *is* it with you? I know there's fire under that ice-princess exterior." He muttered something in Spanish, blew out a breath that screamed frustration, and she suppressed a shiver of delight as it skittered over her skin. He straightened. "Right. Sorry. I'll go say 'hi' to the kids in the practice room and take care of a few things. I'll be back in a little while."

"Thanks."

****

"Who the hell are you?"

So focused on the numbers in front of her, Jade barely suppressed a scream at the unexpected voice. More, she bit back the desire to yell for Han. The girl who stood in the doorway was a fright. Long, dark dreadlocks, questionable tattoos, piercings on her face and ears. A ratty, cut-off t-shirt exposed a belly-button ring that sported a skull. Camo pants were tucked into army boots. Things had taken a decided turn for the worse.

"I'm going over the accounts for Mr. Rivera." Slowly pulling her hands away from the keyboard, Jade hid them in her lap so they wouldn't give away her emotional state.

"Ah, a math whiz," the intruder sneered. "You certainly look the part." She walked in the room and flung herself down in a chair across the desk from her.

Never more grateful to have a desk between her and another person, Jade stiffened and raised one brow. "Did you need something?"

The girl shrugged carelessly, leaned back in her chair and propped her booted feet on the desk. "*Señor* Alejandro lets me hang here on Saturdays. Is he around?"

Interesting. Did the Devil of the Dance Floor have more than a mere philanthropic interest in these kids? "He's in one of the dance studios, I believe. Feel free to go look for him."

She flicked some hair over a shoulder. "Naw. I think I'll just wait here."

So much for concentrating, though she'd figured out the problem. "Don't you want to go practice dancing or something? Isn't that what this place is for?"

She snorted in disgust. "Who said I'm here to

dance? I just hang out, stay out of trouble, blah, blah, blah…"

"Okaay…So you just sit in here?"

"Not always. *Señor* Alejandro's a nice eyeful. I watch him work." The girl's hard, dark eyes gave Jade the once over. "Right now I'm enjoying torturing you. Looks to me like you're out of your comfort zone. Do I scare you?"

"You make me nervous for a lot of reasons I don't want to go into. I'll ignore it if you will."

She laughed and it sounded genuine. "I like you. What's your name?"

Jade wasn't sure if she felt better about that or not, though some of the tension eased from her shoulders. "Jade. Are you going to tell me yours?"

"Not as prissy as you appear." She dropped her feet to the floor with a loud thump and leaned forward, placing her arms on the desk.

Jade's personal space alarms went wild and trying not to be obvious, she leaned back in her chair, rolling it back several inches in the process. It took everything she had not to wince at the loud squeak the wheels made when she did so.

"I'm not making you jumpy, am I?"

"Now why would you think I'm jumpy? I've been leaning over a computer screen for too long. I need to get some kinks out of my back."

She nodded her head once but didn't look like she was buying it. "Cat."

"What did you call me?"

She laughed and the hardness left her eyes. "No, nerd. My name is Cat."

"Ah…That explains one of your tatts then."

"Yes. Evil looking, isn't it?" She held out her arm and looked at the tattoo. "Would you like to know what the other ones are about?"

"No thanks. I have a good imagination. It's enough."

"Let me guess. You have a small heart tattooed somewhere—*private*."

Jade burst out laughing. Now that she had some space and her brain was functioning normally, she was beginning to enjoy the girl. She had a feeling she was more bark than bite. "I like you too, Cat."

"What? Too embarrassed to admit it? It is rather lame."

"I'd have no problem admitting such a thing, if I'd done it. Just not into tattoos."

"Wow. I'll bet you and *Señor* Alejandro are the only people in L.A. who don't have a tattoo."

The information gave her a weird feeling. She wasn't sure if it was a good-weird or a bad-weird. That was two things they had in common. No tattoos and not attached to their cell phones. "Now that's a surprise. I would've expected him to have several." Though now she thought about it, she saw him in nothing but his skivvies and hadn't noticed any. Well, she *had* been stressed at the time.

"Me, too. Said his body was his temple, and he wasn't going to defame it. What's your excuse? Afraid of needles?"

Jade laughed and held out her arms. "If you had beautiful, milky-white skin like this, would you want to ink it up?"

"Oh, spare me! Seriously? You're just chicken."

"Afraid of you taking a punch at me maybe."

Cat made a chicken noise and sat up. "People get worked up by the way I look all the time. What makes you think I even care about your opinion?"

"True. I'm just some white girl from a world completely foreign to you." Jade gave a careless shrug and answered Cat's question. "I don't like them."

"*Órale pues.* Fair enough." She stood. "This conversation is getting boring. I'm going to find *Señor* Alejandro."

Jade logged off the computer and stood as well, resisting the urge to cringe when someone outside the window started yelling in Spanish. She didn't like being so jumpy, and the last thing she wanted was for Cat to notice. "Actually, I'll come with you if you don't mind. I'm not sure where to go, and I need to talk to him."

She followed Cat down the hall, past the reception area where a large, muscular, rather intimidating man sat, looking more like a security guard than a receptionist, and down another short hall where the faint sound of music and a heavy beat could be heard. The volume of the music increased significantly when Cat opened one of the three doors, but the Latin music that was playing wasn't so loud you couldn't speak. They entered a large room with black Marley flooring and a wall made entirely of mirrors. It reflected a group of about twenty teenagers, mostly girls, practicing a variety of moves while Han prowled around giving pointers.

Cat boldly entered and crossed the room to sit against a wall. Jade closed the door behind her and leaned against it, feeling like an intruder. As she watched Han, she was surprised at how comfortable he was among dancers of any level—even with the impediment of his injured wrist—and by how good he was with the kids. Under-privileged, neglected teenagers who loved to dance, some of them with undeniable talent and others who simply enjoyed the chance to learn. Where did Cat belong in all this?

The side of dance-instructor Han was completely different from the one she'd seen on television. He wasn't barking orders, demanding perfection and forcing the students to position their bodies exactly the way he deemed necessary. His words were encouraging, his body relaxed, his expression...

Wow. So much emotion on that face. Friendliness, concern, sympathy, a desire to help in any way he could. This was not the man from television, nor the one of the last twenty-four hours. This man gave his soul to these kids, anxious for them to succeed. Her heart opened a bit and an unfamiliar emotion seeped in. A warmth swirled through her entire being. She clenched her teeth and hardened her heart. She would not let herself feel such things about a man, any man.

Entirely absorbed in the whole scenario, Jade had no idea how long she stood there before Han walked over. He placed himself between her and the rest of the room, respecting her need for distance, but making it impossible for her to look at anything but him.

"You're welcome to join in. No experience necessary. It might even give you a head start on our lessons."

Shaking her head, she gave him a half-smile. "I don't think so. I'm out of place enough as it is."

He shrugged. "You underestimate yourself, I think. I see you've met Cat."

"Yes. Now there's an experience. Apparently she's

here for the eye candy."

"*Como?*"

"Nothing. She said you let her hang out here and watch. She's not interested in dancing."

He blew out a breath that screamed frustration. "Oh, she's interested. She just has huge barriers up right now. I'm trying to breach them."

He brushed his hair back off his forehead, and a desire to be the one running her fingers through his hair caught her by surprise. She focused on the beat of the music and muted chatter of the students instead, looking at his chin rather than in his eyes.

"Did you find anything in the accounts?"

"Yes, I figured out the problem, though it's going to take a little work to get it straightened out. I'd like to load everything on a flash drive and work on it at my office. If you're interested in hiring me to fix it that is. Otherwise, I can show you what's going on, and you can take care of it yourself."

He nodded. "*Si.* I will take a look and then decide how I want to handle it." He looked over at Cat who was watching them. "You know, if you get out on the floor and learn some dance moves, Cat might give it a try. Her mother is an exotic dancer, and I think that might be what's put her off the concept. My gut tells me she's got some real talent. I'm running out of ways to try and get her to do more than watch."

"That sounds like a challenge. Let me see what I can do. I learned some tricks with Lexi."

The look of relief that crossed his face at her offer made her warm to him even more. He sincerely cared about helping Cat. His gesture of letting her hang out in the studio was rooted in more than a humanitarian need to share some of his wealth with the less fortunate. Until he squashed it all with one fast comment.

"Better than joining me on the dance floor and having me *touch* you, isn't it?"

"Go to hell, Han." She marched across the room to Cat, collapsed on the floor next to her and called him a few foul names under her breath.

"I certainly hope you're not talking to me," the girl said. "Generally, I bash a person's face in after that kind of comment."

"Alejandro Rivera."

"That's almost as bad. *Señor* Alejandro's amazing."

"To you maybe. He wants me to join the class and learn a few dance moves. The last thing I need is to make a fool of myself in front of a bunch of teenagers. He lets you hang out here and do nothing. I don't know why he has to hassle me to get out there. I'm just here to fix his accounting problem."

"Knew you were a chicken."

Jade shrugged carelessly. "I'll own it. When it comes to dancing, I'm a chicken. The last thing I ever want to do is dance in front of people. At least I'm not pretending I'm only here to enjoy the Latin eye-candy." She leaned back on her elbows and stretched her legs out in front of her, then pretended she was ogling Han as he demonstrated a dance move, while a nearby couple gave them a hard time. "I think you're the one that's chicken. Too afraid of what people might think if you enjoyed it. Or maybe you really suck at it, and you're too scared to let everyone know it."

Cat snorted in disgust. "You are so lame. Do I look like I'd be afraid of anything?"

"I think you want people to think you're not afraid when you really are."

"Well, nerd," Cat sneered and started unlacing her boots, "Let me show you how unafraid I am. I can make these wannabes look like they have no idea what they're doing."

Jade smothered a laugh when she saw the shocked expression on Han's face as Cat approached with the demand he dance with her.

She thoroughly enjoyed the show—as per usual whenever she watched Alejandro Rivera dance—for several minutes before quietly letting herself out of the room and heading back to the office for another look at the accounts. With Cat finally joining the class, it might be a while before Han was ready to leave. Hopefully it would distract her from the warm, fuzzy feeling she got when he mouthed '*Thank you*' to her over Cat's shoulder. And do a better job of it than the number puzzles had earlier. If she could focus and finish the job, she wouldn't have to worry about taking the work back to her office. The last thing she needed was another reason to spend time with a man she couldn't want.

****

With a sigh of relief, Jade clicked print, then raised both hands over her head and stretched. She'd done it. Standing up, she bent forward, back and then side to side with her hands braced in the small of her back. It felt really good to solve the puzzle of Han's accounts, but not so good to straighten up from bending forward and look directly into a pair of topaz eyes, gleaming with appreciation. She hated when men looked at her like that.

Didn't she?

"You look pretty satisfied with yourself. Did you solve my problem?"

"Printing it off right now. It looks like the previous owner of your company was a tax evader. I hope he didn't rip you off too, when he sold you the place."

"I minored in business, remember?"

She raised her brows in question. "All right then."

He scowled. "What's the problem?"

She took the stack of papers from the printer, then sat back down at the desk. Motioning Han into the seat on the other side, she turned the pages so they were right side up for him. "Clever bit of work, but not too hard to figure out or fix, if you're looking for it. This is a copy of your accounts. Notice how every month there's a donation, always the same amount?"

"*Sí*, but that is nothing. The previous owner said he donated from the profits of Seriously Dance every month because it helped Let's Dance stay open and worked as a tax write off for him. Also, it didn't hurt Seriously Dance because the studio was doing so well, and it always operated in the black."

"Yes, I guessed as much. However, look at how much comes out in expenses for Let's Dance over the next two weeks."

"Hmmm…" The room was quiet for a moment as he went over the figures. "It is the exact same amount that went in."

"Yes. Every month it goes in and goes back out under the guise of expenses. Rather vague, don't you think? And just looking at this place, I'd say that much money is not being spent here every month. Things would be a lot nicer if they were."

"No kidding."

"You want to know where the 'expense' money went?"

"Let me guess, the owner's bank account."

She chuckled. "Not quite as obvious as that. I looked through the bills, and there are several every month to Seriously Dance for supplies with nothing itemized, so there's no way to tell what was purchased from the other studio. I'd like to have a look at Seriously Dance's books to see how they covered up that end of it. I have no idea what they'd be purchasing from the other studio, but you could check inventory to see if anything corresponds there."

He swore under his breath. "What a mess. I'd love you to look over all of it. I will pay you, of course." He ran a hand around the back of his neck and squeezed his eyes shut for a moment. "The absolute last thing I want is to screw around with the IRS. Whatever you need to do to straighten out this mess, do it." He slapped his good hand on the table and stood. "Shall we head over to Seriously Dance now, and you can check out those accounts?"

"Since it involves working, I'd just as soon load it all on a flash drive and take a look at it in my office on Monday. It's Saturday, Han. I don't work on weekends."

"Sorry. I've worked weekends for so long, I forget most people don't." He gathered up the papers she'd printed for him, put them in a file cabinet and locked it. "Shall we go?"

Chapter Six

A frown marred Han's forehead as he stood at the floor-to-ceiling surveillance mirror in his office and watched Jade pace from one end of the dance studio to the other. The mirror was concealed among a wall of mirrors in the dance studio where Jade paced.

He clasped his hands behind his back and tapped his foot a few times. He routinely observed new students without their knowledge before he worked with them. It helped determine what kind of music got them moving; then once they were moving, gauge how much dance experience and natural talent they had.

With Jade, the music was doing nothing for her, the look on her face telling him she'd rather be anywhere but there. Though when something came on she liked, she would tap her foot to the beat. Still, none of it was enough to make her forget why she was there. Even from his vantage point, he could sense her tension. He knew teaching her would be a challenge, which was why he grilled Lexi about her favorite music, in case he needed to play it.

A good fifteen minutes had elapsed since she arrived, and all he learned was how annoyed she was with the wait. Understandable. She was probably scared, freaked out about the situation, and desperate to get it over. He sighed. Time to play something he knew she'd like. Contemporary music. Who knew? He figured her to be more of a jazz or blues type. Although she did like some of the modern singing artists who had a vintage sound which didn't surprise him.

He walked over to the stereo system, set it to play five of her favorite songs with a fast beat. He hoped like hell he wouldn't have to wait through all five to see if she was inspired to move.

When he returned to his observation post, she was seated on a bench with her head back against the wall, eyes closed, her fingers playing with the locket around her neck. He frowned. Wearing a necklace during a dance lesson wasn't a good idea.

Then the music he'd programmed began to play, and he had to pick his jaw up off the floor. Her tension drained away and was non-existent before the first song was half over and by the end Jade was tapping her foot to the beat and singing the lyrics. At least, he assumed she was singing since he couldn't actually hear her. When the next song came on, she hopped off the bench and moved around to the music. Just what he hoped to see. What he hadn't expected was the natural grace and complete lack of inhibition he saw in her movements. And how quickly watching her move heated his blood. Now *that* would be a problem.

He canceled the rest of the songs in the lineup and waited until the one playing finished before he left the office and headed to the studio. If he walked in while she was still dancing, his job would be even more of a challenge. He didn't need anything else added to the mountain he had to climb with her.

****

What was taking Han so long? She wanted the lesson over; the wait drove her up a wall. It was a blessed relief when her favorite singing artist started to play over the speakers. Just the distraction she needed, and by the time the second song came on, she decided a few Zumba moves would relieve her tension. She loved dancing, and her exercise of choice was the Latin-based dance-exercise. Not that she needed the exercise to keep her figure—she'd never worried about that—but working at a desk made her feel the need to release some energy at the end of the day.

When the song was over and nothing started to play after it, she went back to the bench and sat down. Before the tension had a chance to build again, Han entered the room. She didn't know which was harder, trying to avoid acting all googly-eyed at the way he looked, or the fact it was time to start the lesson.

No one had a right to look so good in a white V-neck t-shirt and gray sweatpants. Not much different than the gray yoga capris and the pink tank top she had on. Comfortable clothes that were easy to move in. But he looked *so* good in something so ordinary. Was it the bracelets he wore on his uninjured arm? Several colorful beaded ones made of round wooden and glass beads, as well as the same platinum, chunky chain he'd worn at dinner. They definitely added to the overall picture. And his bandaged wrist gave him just a touch of vulnerability, so she didn't feel quite so intimidated by whom she was actually taking dance lessons from.

She sighed. It was just *him*. It didn't matter what he wore; he rocked it. Well, the dark chest hair peeking out of the vee of his shirt might factor in there, too.

"Ready to get to work?"

"As I'll ever be, I suppose." She stood and wiped sweaty hands on her pants. "You need to know, I've never danced with anyone before. I have no clue what I'm doing."

He bobbed his head. "I'm excited about the challenge. First thing, though, you need to take off the necklace. One or both of us can get hit in the face with it."

She felt the color drain from her face.

The stress of what was to come made her touchstone invaluable. Could she do it?

Most of the time, over the last few years, she forgot it hung around her neck. It took more than a year after she finished therapy for her to stop depending on it when things got stressful. Since meeting Han last week, she started needing it regularly again. In the end, it came down to the lesser of two evils: admitting to this man why she needed to wear it—or going without it in a situation that could send her into a tailspin.

No. She was strong now. Nothing was going to send her over the edge. She was fine. She could do this. Han had proved she could trust him. His touch felt good. There was no reason to panic. She pulled the necklace over her head and dropped it in her hand. She closed her fingers around it and shut her eyes as she held it tight for several seconds before setting it down on the bench next to her car keys, water bottle, and cell phone. She turned to face Han, determined not to let him see how hard that one little step was.

"Good. All set?" At her nod, he continued, "Do you know the song Lexi has picked out for our dance?"

"Last time I talked to her, she hadn't settled on one yet. I do know their song is one of Ed Sheeran's, her favorite singer."

"Yes. They'll be doing a waltz. For us, it will be a

foxtrot to one of Maroon 5's songs."

Relief washed through her. They weren't doing a sexy Latin number. She clenched and unclenched her hands. She could do this. It would get her past her phobia once and for all. A test of sorts: being up close and personal to someone besides her sister, without having a panic attack. She already knew Han's touch didn't make her skin crawl. She'd been as close to him as she'd ever been to a man since…

Don't think about him now.

She broke out in a nervous sweat. Was she going to freak out like she usually did when a man got too close? Or would she go to the other extreme and do something crazy like when she kissed him in the elevator? She wiped her hands on her hips and clasped them behind her back.

"This makes you happy?" he asked. "You like the foxtrot? You know something about it?"

She squared her shoulders. Time to come clean about her secret indulgence. "I'm going to tell you something, but it's only because I'd do anything for my sister. It is the last thing I'd want to admit to you."

His jaw clenched. "*Gracias.* I appreciate the compliment."

She let out a frustrated sigh, unclasped her hands, and went to run her fingers through her hair. She dropped them when she remembered it was in a braid. "I'm a huge fan of your dance competition program and have watched it since day one. I know a lot about dancing; I've just never danced with another person before."

Something that looked suspiciously like satisfaction flashed in his eyes, but his face remained impassive. "Are you telling me you're a fan of *mine*?"

As much as she hated to admit it…She shrugged and turned away from him, put a foot up on the bench and pretended to tighten her shoe lace. "Just laying things out on the table." She dropped her foot and turned back to him, her composure restored. "You need to get over yourself. I know a lot about different kinds of dance from watching your program for so long." She threw back her shoulders, raised her arms to chest level, bent at the elbows with one palm facing down and the other hand raised. She tilted her head back and turned it to the side. "Ballroom dance frame."

He nodded his head once. "*Bueno*. You have the idea, but it needs a little work." He stepped closer, put his palms on her elbows and raised them higher. She managed to keep herself from jumping at his touch, but she couldn't help the slight twitch. Which he noticed, of course.

He frowned. "I am hoping with practice you will get used to me touching you, and it will become commonplace. I'm warning you now, there is going to be a lot of touching."

She gave him a look that said, *I'm not an idiot,* and he moved from standing in front of her to standing behind her. Her breath came out in a whoosh, and she jumped when his hands descended on her shoulders and pulled them back. She was grateful he ignored her reaction.

"You need to lean back from your partner slightly." He placed one hand on her stomach, the other in the small of her back and straightened her stance. "Your frame needs to be locked."

Please don't let him feel how hard my heart is

pounding.

And it wasn't with fear. Well, maybe it was, but it was a different fear than she usually experienced. She was afraid of how good his hands felt and how much she wanted them stay right where they were. She was also afraid of disappointing him. Of not dancing to his standards. Of making him regret the gift he was giving Lexi and Beck.

"I hope doing that didn't hurt your wrist. Is it healing all right?"

"It's much better than last time I saw you, and I'm an expert at working with injuries, so don't give it another thought." He stepped back from her and swept a hand in the direction of the mirrored wall. "Take a long look at how you need to hold yourself for this dance. Memorize the look and feel." He paused for several long moments. "*Sí.* You can relax." He stepped behind her, put his hands on her hips and propelled her forward. "Let's move to the middle of the floor and I will show you the first basic steps." Once there, he let go of her and moved away. "Back in frame."

His bossy tone grated, but she did as he said. And she did it perfectly. Though what she really wanted was to stand there and admire the way he looked in the mirror.

"Technically, my moves are the opposite of yours. For now, I will do your moves standing next to you and you copy me. *Sí?*"

"Do you want me to watch you or the mirror?"

"Mirror. We are going to start with the right foot, taking two steps back on your toes and dragging the heel of your left foot as you bring it back next to your other foot. Like this."

He demonstrated the move smoothly and effortlessly. It felt awkward when she did it, but it didn't look as bad as it felt when she watched herself in the mirror.

He nodded. "Not bad for your first try. Now, a sidestep to the right. Do it with me and watch in the mirror. Then we'll go up to the mirror and practice it several times across the room. The rhythm is slow, slow, quick, quick."

The steps were easy enough to get the hang of. Keeping the frame was the more difficult task, made more stressful when he grabbed her from behind like he had the first time, putting one hand on her stomach and one on her back to push her into position. They repeated the steps over and over across the length of the room until they had nowhere to go.

"Go back to the mirror and I will watch this time," he instructed. "You need to do it until it comes naturally and you don't think about it."

After what felt like forever, he called a halt. The muscles in her arms and abdomen burned. All she wanted was to sit and take a long swig of water. And the next time he barked the word *frame* at her, she might just haul off and punch him in the nose.

After she quenched her thirst, he announced, "Now we do it together."

Her stomach sank. This was the part she'd worried about most. Being held. By someone stronger and bigger than her. Penned in by a muscular body on one side and strong arms on the other. Just thinking about it had her on the verge of hyperventilating. She raised her hand to her neck. *Damn.* She closed her eyes for a moment. She'd been trapped between him and the wall of the elevator *and liked it.* This was no different than then. This was Han and she liked him and his proximity.

Relax and enjoy the once-in-a-lifetime opportunity of dancing with The Alejandro Rivera.

"Are you okay? Did I push you too hard? It's a bit of a learning curve for me in the first couple of lessons too, figuring out what my student is capable of. What they can handle. How much is too much."

She nodded, appreciating the concern in his voice and expression. *Just suck it up and do it, Jade. This isn't your stepfather.* In an effort to block out memories which hadn't plagued her in years and the *feelings* that had resurfaced, she stood. "Let's do it."

When he took her hand in his, she clenched her jaw, but when the bandaged one rested on her back she twitched. No way he hadn't felt that. *Damn it.* She looked in the mirror. It was a reflection of her with *Alejandro Rivera. Not* her stepfather. Her heart rate slowed, and her jaw muscles relaxed, but she couldn't completely release her tension.

"You need to figure out how to relax. You are wound up far too tight to do this anywhere close to right. I am not trying to be sexual. I'm teaching you how to dance the foxtrot. Now, ballroom frame."

She let out a little laugh, which released some tension. "I swear to God, you say frame one more time, and you will regret it."

She felt the chuckle rumble in his chest. The pressure of his hand on her back increased significantly, and he countered the pressure of his hand with his hips this time instead of his other hand, so that her frame locked into position. He let go of her hand, took hold of her chin and turned her head to one side. "Frame."

She stomped on his foot. Not hard, as a joke more than anything, but she *had* warned him. He let out a few Spanish expletives under his breath. *Oops*.

"Do that again and you will be the one regretting things. You will be stepping on my toes unintentionally more times than you or I can keep track of. I don't need you doing it on purpose. Now, right foot back. Ready? *Go*. Slow, slow, quick, quick. Again."

This was so much worse—and so much better— than she feared. With every step back, his leg came between hers, his hand lightly pressed into her back and his voice rumbled through her chest. One minute she was reveling in the feel of him, the next she was having an ugly flashback. And the whole time she had to remember she was dancing, that her feet needed to follow the steps. She tried desperately to hang onto her composure, to concentrate on what her body was supposed to be doing, but by the time they made it across the room she couldn't control her shaking. She broke out of his hold and walked rapidly to the bench and sat down, wishing there was a hole she could crawl into. She was such a freak. He was merely dancing with her. She bowed her head and put her hands over her face. *Pull yourself together, Jade.* She dropped her hands and picked up the necklace, tracing the locket's design with her thumb, her eyes on Han. He was leaning against the wall, legs crossed at the ankles, arms crossed over his chest.

"Would you believe me if I said I just need to rest for a minute?"

"No. But I will if you want me to."

He let out a resigned sigh, pushed away from the

wall and walked over to sit next to her, careful to leave a good amount of space between them. His eyes flicked to her hands before resting on her face.

"Maybe you should tell your sister you can't do this. There's no rule that says without a wedding party dance the bride and groom aren't married."

Her eyes filled with tears and her nose tickled as she attempted a smile. She sniffed and blinked several times to get rid of it. "I can't, Han. I *can't.*"

"She'll understand. Does she have any idea what this is doing to you?"

"She has no idea *how* hard it is." She looked at the locket. "I can't do it to her."

"Why? Just because she's your sister doesn't mean you have to give her whatever she wants."

"Oh, I know that. I had the joy of raising her through her teen years. She's heard 'no' from me more times than you can count."

"So, what's one more then?"

"It's her wedding, Han. And she's marrying a wonderful man. I want it to be perfect, probably more than she does. She deserves it. And it's already not perfect because she doesn't have a father to walk her down the aisle. Which in a way is my fault. So I owe her this."

"And now we get to the crux of the matter. How is her having no father your fault?"

Her hand clenched tightly around the locket and she ground her teeth together to keep herself from opening the locket and looking at the picture of Lexi. Her ears started ringing, and she squeezed her eyes shut for a moment, fighting the urge to run. She needed to act normal. As though his question wasn't a big deal.

"What does any of it have to do with my learning how to dance?"

He looked at her in silence for a heartbeat. "You're going to have to take my word for it when I say it has everything to do with it, and if you seriously want to do this for your sister's wedding, you're going to have to let me know exactly what is going on. So I can do what I can to help."

She jumped up and walked to the door. So much for acting like it wasn't a big deal. No way she was talking to him about this. She hadn't talked to anyone other than her therapist about it. Lexi knew some of it because she had been with her when it was going on and seen things, but she'd never *talked* to her. About any of it. At the sound of his voice, her hand on the door knob, she froze, her back to him.

"My mother was a prostitute. She was beat to death by her pimp when I was five and my brother was ten." He stated it like he was reciting a math equation. "So my brother and I ended up living on the streets of San Juan, performing for the tourists on the cruise ships that docked there. I would dance, and my brother would play the harmonica, hoping they would give us some money for our efforts."

Her shoulders slumped as she turned to face him. "Oh my God. I don't even know what to say to that." She slowly walked back and sat next to him.

"No one knows this. My bio for public consumption is mostly fiction. So I'm taking a great risk telling you this. I'm doing it because it's vital for you to trust me."

Her breath caught in her throat; her heart pounded like a base drum for a couple beats. That was huge.

Letting the cat out of the bag and having the public know he was claustrophobic made him a quirky celebrity. Letting them know about his childhood would be a major humiliation for him. And he told her anyway. She rested her elbows on her knees, locket clutched tightly in one hand, and stared at her feet.

"I won't tell anyone, Han," she said softly. "And I'll tell you mine. If you really think it will help. If I even can." She looked up over her shoulder at him. "How much time is left?"

"I have nothing scheduled after you. We have as much time as it takes." The corner of his mouth quirked up. "I had a feeling this would be complicated."

She continued to stare at her feet as though they could give her the strength she needed, then opened her fist and looked at the locket, ran her thumb over its surface. Her heart started thundering in her chest. He wasn't the first stranger she'd told. Just the first man. She looked at the locket, imagining the picture that rested inside. *Lexi.* She refused to let her stepfather have any more power over her, and she certainly wasn't going to let him ruin Lexi's wedding day.

"My mother died when I was seventeen. In a car accident. My stepfather inherited the responsibility of caring for us by default, since our biological father was in prison. When my mom was alive, it wasn't a big deal. He was an okay stepdad. He was desperately in love with her but rather ambivalent toward us. For him, it was all about my mother; Lexi and I happened to be part of the deal. And he gave my mom a good life. They were happy. So I am grateful for that." She stopped and squeezed her eyes shut.

"So what happened, *chica?*" he asked softly, and

that delicious Spanish accent released some of her tension.

Now for the hard part. "Nothing out of the ordinary to begin with. He started drinking to cope. A little bit at first but it escalated. He never drank at work, but it got to the point where he was trashed the rest of the time."

She found herself drifting into the memory and forgetting Han was there as she talked. That it felt good to tell him came as a surprise. Even more surprising, she was telling this to *Alejandro Rivera*.

"I came home later than usual from work one night. Normally I worked a few hours after school and was home in time to make dinner, but it was tax season, a few days before the deadline, so I got home long after Lexi was in bed. My stepfather was drunk as usual and followed me into the kitchen when I went to get something for dinner."

She went to run a hand through her hair and was frustrated by the French braid again. Irritated, she yanked the band off the end and ran a hand through her hair to loosen it. Then she continued with the hardest part of the story. "He—ah—came up behind me, called me by my mother's name, and pulled me back against him. It caught me by surprise, so I didn't pull away. Then he ran his hands all over the front of me. And I mean *all over*." She paused and bit her lip, suppressing a shiver of revulsion. "I caught him by surprise and escaped his hold. That was when he saw I wasn't my mother. He apologized profusely and went to his room." She sucked in a deep breath, only then realizing she needed it.

When the silence dragged on, Han said, "There's more."

She nodded. "About a week later he did the same thing, only this time, he knew exactly who I was. For weeks we did a grab and dodge routine, and it felt like he was putting his hands on me all the time. He probably wasn't, but it got magnified in my head and wore me out."

With a shudder, she jumped to her feet and walked forward a few paces, arms wrapped around her middle. She took a couple deep breaths, started to speak, then stopped. Only by keeping her back to Han was she finally able to blurt it out. "One night, he climbed into my bed."

She ground her teeth together. Han was right. She needed to say this. She had this weird sense he wanted to protect her and make it better. And she longed for that, even though it was stupid to think it, much less want it. She needed to be able to dance at her sister's wedding, but more importantly, she needed to get over this phobia completely, to stop letting her stepfather dictate her life. And maybe, just maybe, getting it out there, verbalizing it, would help her finish the last bit of her healing.

"He pulled me to him so my back was against his chest and his hands went under my shirt…" She shuddered and after taking a moment to compose herself, she continued, "He held me so tight, I couldn't get away, and I could feel every inch of him along the back of me. He was—he was…" Her voice lost its strength and she cleared her throat.

"Happy to see you?" Han supplied.

She nodded. "I *hated* it. The way it felt, what it meant. And his hands where touching me everywhere. I swear, the guy was an octopus or something." She shuddered again.

She heard Han jump to his feet, and she turned to see him pace across the room and back. A sleek jungle panther on the prowl for prey. Her eyes couldn't look anywhere else when he did it again. Then he stopped a few feet away, hands fisted at his sides, body rigid. Through clenched teeth he asked, "Did he rape you?"

Suddenly her eyes were filled with tears; they dripped down her cheeks. *Where the hell had they come from?* Her throat felt so tight she couldn't speak so she shook her head.

The tension drained from him as he muttered, *"Gracias a Dios."* He blew out a breath. "What stopped him?"

"He was drunk," she whispered; she didn't have the strength to speak any louder. Swiping the back of her hands across her cheeks, she went to the bench and collapsed on it. She cleared her throat. "He passed out. After that night, I slept with Lexi in her room. I was so scared he'd try something with her, never mind me, again. I found him passed out in my bed a few times after that, and he still used every opportunity to touch me. After I graduated a few months later, I moved out and took Lexi with me. We haven't seen him since. Lexi has been the only one whose touch doesn't make my skin crawl."

He sat down next to her and after a lengthy silence took her hand in his. "This makes your skin crawl?"

She looked at their joined hands. Dare she tell him? She was deathly afraid of the power it would give him. A tremor ran through her at the thought, and he dropped her hand.

"It does."

For Lexi, remember? "No, Han. I've seen a therapist for this, so I'm at peace with things now." She held up her locket. "I use this to ground me, remind me I'm in the present, not with him anymore. That he has no power to hurt me. But now...I have no problem with your touching me and that scares me."

He put a finger under her chin and gently turned her face toward him. "I'm glad. It means the rest will come. You have natural talent and if you can get past your phobia, you will rock this thing and give your sister an awesome wedding gift." He kissed her lips softly and quickly, then removed his finger to lean back against the wall. He closed his eyes and took a deep breath.

"The way you make me feel scares me to death, too."

She stifled a groan. She didn't need to know that. It was too much right now. Her heart pounded hard in her chest for several beats, and she took a calming breath. She decided to ignore the comment.

"So now what?"

"So, now I know what I'm dealing with, maybe we can make some progress. Let's try dancing together again." He reached over and touched the chain of the locket that dangled outside of her fist. "You can wear this. Any damage it may do, I'm sure we'll survive. I think it will help more than it may hurt." He stood and held his hand out to her.

She put the necklace on, then took his hand as her heart started its pounding rhythm again and stood as well.

He didn't let go of her hand as pulled her to the center of the room. Without coming any closer, he put his other hand on her hip, leaving a good distance between them so that the only place he was touching her was her hand and hip. Just as she was about to relax in relief, he ordered, "Put your hand on my shoulder and get in frame."

She did as he said and something of what she was thinking must have shown on her face.

"You better not try anything. You want me to stop saying 'frame', then you need to do it without a reminder. Now, we can dance without touching more than we are now until you are ready to get closer, but you need to know that you will have to get ready. You want to do this, then you need to wrap your head around that. Now, we dance. Slow, slow, quick, quick."

****

He didn't want to think about his mother. He didn't want to think about what that bastard did to Jade. And what did he do to keep from thinking? He danced. So he'd barked orders and moved Jade around the dance floor for a good hour before she complained.

"That's it, you sadist. I've had enough. Push me for as long as you want, but that's as good as it's going to get today. I'm *done*."

She pulled away from him, grabbed a towel from the shelf by the door and sat on the bench as she wiped the sweat from her face, neck and arms. Once done, she set the towel on the bench, grabbed her water bottle and took a long swig. "Now I know why they call you the Devil of the Dance Floor. Hot, sexy and oh so *evil*."

He grinned. And told himself he did not want to be the one drying off her sweaty body. Teaching her to dance was enough of a complication. Breaking down her barriers to the point she'd have sex with him? Not worth it. He knew plenty of women willing to take care of that particular itch who weren't anywhere near the amount of work.

"Shall we pick up some takeout and go to my house? We can eat on my patio, listen to the surf, enjoy the sunset, swim if you'd like and pamper our sore muscles in my hot tub."

She looked at him like he'd lost his mind; he suppressed a grin. "Don't worry, I'm not trying to seduce you. It's all part of my plan. Teaching you to dance perfectly is going to take more than just learning some steps in a dance studio. I need you relaxed around me. I don't want to have to start from scratch again at our next lesson. So, more time together after the progress we've made is a good idea."

"Slave driver."

The words might've been harsh if they hadn't been accompanied by the slight upward tilt of her mouth and a sparkle in her eyes.

He nodded his head once and suppressed a smile. He was the one in charge here. "*Gracias*. You're learning, *chica*." He took her towel, as well as the one he'd used to wipe himself down with, and threw them in a bin, then grabbed her hands and pulled her to her feet. "We've got showers here, so let's get cleaned up, and I'll meet you out in the parking lot."

She relaxed into him when he wrapped an arm around her waist. She didn't flinch or pull away, and he smiled at the progress. He clenched his jaw for a moment then forced himself to relax. He was *not* happy about that for any other reason than he was her teacher, and he'd made a breakthrough. When they reached the door, he opened it for her and kept his hand in the small of her back as he followed her through it. After he closed the door behind them, he returned his hand to her waist and pulled her next to him. He felt her tremble. It crossed his mind it was because he hadn't broken through her barriers after all, before he sensed it was something altogether different. Something he was feeling too.

He looked down at her and thoroughly enjoyed the view. The creamy skin of her long neck made him suppress the urge to taste it. The curves displayed by the scooped neckline of her top captured his gaze for several moments before he stopped in his tracks. His fingers tightened on her waist and they stopped. She looked up at him questioningly. He reached out with his bandaged hand and tucked her bra strap back underneath her tank top.

"Is red secretly your favorite color?"

What he saw in her eyes at his touch stilled him momentarily, his finger pressed against her skin under the strap. Slowly, caressingly, he removed it and ran his finger up her neck, along her jaw, to stop at the corner of her mouth. His heart thundered in his chest making his body throb as the blood pulsed through it. Hers was the loveliest mouth he'd ever seen and to curb the impulse to devour that mouth, he lightly ran his finger across her bottom lip. When he traced it back across, her tongue came out, and he wondered if was to rid her mouth of the feel of his finger or get a taste of him.

Then his brain turned off and other parts of him had his head bending down and his tongue coming out to touch hers. He pulled his head back at the last second, before he made contact. As he hustled her down the hallway he didn't know which was worse, how quickly she turned him on, or the foreign feelings that coursed through him. Feelings that weren't related to sexual pleasure and more about how *she* was feeling, what *she* needed. So much more personal than the pleasure of the moment. He squirmed in his skin.

"Yes."

He halted abruptly and when his fingers dug into her waist, he felt her stiffen. "Yes, what?"

"Red is my favorite color."

He bent his head down and whispered in her ear, "Mine, too. How long is it going to take you to get clean?"

He felt a shiver snake through her. The reaction he hoped for. He shouldn't be so pleased with the fact it took a moment for her to answer, but he liked knowing he did that to her. He also liked how she stood up to him and gave as good as she got when the occasion called for it. He caught his breath. He liked that she treated him like a regular guy and not a celebrity. He wanted to squirm in his skin again with that thought because he enjoyed women treating him like royalty. Was it because it filled a need his mother hadn't? *Not the time or the place for psychoanalysis, Rivera.*

"Fifteen minutes tops."

He nodded. "Here we are. This is the women's. I'll see you in a few."

When she threw an arm around his neck, threaded her fingers through his hair and pulled his head towards her, he momentarily stiffened with shock before he gave in to her demand. She captured his mouth in a kiss that left him reeling and disappeared behind the door of the women's locker room before he had a chance to respond.

He collapsed against the wall next to the door of the men's locker room. That was twice now she'd kissed him. He was in serious trouble. He wanted her so much it hurt. He couldn't recall ever wanting a woman that badly. Much less after only a kiss. He clenched his fists, then bit back a groan when it painfully reminded him of his injury. Giving in to the desire to bash his fist into something, he slammed it against the door to the men's locker room as he pushed it open. Hard enough it banged against the wall. *Damn it!* He'd never needed a cold shower after a dance lesson before. And all it took was a quick, *chaste* kiss.

As he exited the building twenty minutes later, she surprised him again. Not only was she ready before him, she was leaning against a small red convertible. And she looked *hot*.

"That's your car?"

She gave him a mischievous grin. "Indeed. You don't like it?"

He shook his head. "You never cease to surprise me. I figured on the red, since you said it was your favorite color, but was thinking more along the lines of something practical, like a Japanese hybrid." His expression must have given away his shock because she laughed. So he shrugged a shoulder to appear careless.

"Of course. A boring, accountant-type car. Actually, I have a silver one of those I use for work. Gives the right impression to my clients. Not that I drive to my clients very often, but it looks good sitting in front of the office."

"That fits. An environmentally conscientious accountant." He jangled his keys on the end of his finger. "You want to follow me to the house, and we'll have some food delivered there?"

She shrugged a shoulder. "Up to you, boss."

Whether it was to remind herself or him this was just business, it did a good job putting his head back where it belonged. She'd probably kissed him in an attempt to get past her issues, nothing more. He wanted to bang his head on a wall to make that sink in. He didn't need anything else from her. *Did not.* There were plenty of other fish in the sea, and he was pretty sure after tonight he was going to need to call one of his many fish. For a reality check. To get his perspective back.

Chapter Seven

"So, do you enjoy your work?" Han asked as they relaxed on the loveseat on his flagstone patio, enjoying a glass of wine and the sunset as he'd promised.

She took a sip of expensive merlot, settled more deeply into the red cushions of the wicker loveseat, and contemplated his question. "For the most part. I enjoy playing with numbers, though some of it is boring and routine. Sniffing out the problem with your books was a treat I don't get too often. Lately I've been thinking about working as a forensic accountant. It would be challenging and fun, but it's a huge step from where I'm at right now, and I'm not quite ready to do it."

He groaned. "My God, you just said accounting was fun. I've been around more than my share of women and not a single one would ever say math was fun. It intrigues me..." He cleared his throat. "For a while I knew I wanted to have my own dance studio, as well as work with underprivileged children, but it was several years before I was in a place where I was ready for the change."

"Had you worked with children before you bought Let's Dance?"

"*Si.* Occasionally. Volunteer work."

"Is that what made you realize you want to do it?"

He went silent and for several moments the only sound was the surf. Which made the sudden squawk of a gull unnaturally loud.

He put his arm around her and pulled her to him, and it wasn't until she rested her head on his shoulder that she realized the length of his thigh resting against hers and his arm across her shoulders didn't freak her out. It felt natural and right. But rather than analyze it like the accountant side of her wanted to, she decided to merely enjoy the moment. Good God, had she ever done that before? *No. No. Not analyzing anything.*

"No, *chica.*"

He spoke softly but his tension was palpable. Why would talking about his volunteer work wind him up so tight? Her muscles tensed in response. Was he going to tell her? Should she ask? Did she even want to know? Suddenly it was personal, maybe too personal, and it made her uncomfortable. She didn't do personal. Especially not with a man.

"I decided to do that when Marguerite died."

She clenched her teeth, then let her breath out slowly when she realized what she was doing. "Marguerite?" She prayed there was nothing in her voice other than curiosity, because he sure as hell didn't need to know a pang of jealousy shot through her.

"My—what was the phrase you used?—*Sugar Mama.*"

She groaned. "Just let that go, would you? I was totally stressed out that night."

She desperately wanted to pull away from him, climb into her safe little personal-space bubble. Could he tell her heart was pounding? Did he feel her muscles sag with relief when he told her who Marguerite was? She did not need to care so much about the women in his past. It was the road to heartache. The man had been with more women than the amount of men she'd merely talked to. And most of her clients were men.

"Marguerite was probably the closest thing I ever had to a mother or a father."

"Did she adopt you and your brother?"

His fingers tightened on her shoulder for a moment, and she was surprised at her reaction to the slightly aggressive action. She didn't panic; she didn't have the urge to get away from his hold. She merely felt uncomfortable at the momentary pain and relieved when he loosened his grip. And glad he didn't remove his arm. Which was seriously stupid. A moment ago, she wanted to get away from him

She lifted her head off his shoulder and when she looked at his face, she could just make out his indecisive expression in the fading light. Softly she told him, "You don't have to answer that if you don't want."

"Maybe you're not the only one here who needs to learn some trust."

"What do you mean?"

He gave a self-deprecating smile. "You have man issues; I have woman issues."

"Your mother?" she guessed, because it can't have been good to have a prostitute for a mother.

She felt his entire body go rock hard and realized he'd probably felt her sag with relief moments before. *Damn it.* Up close and personal was complicated. Avoiding it was a good thing in a lot of ways.

"Women are for dancing with, playing with, having fun with, having sex with. Not for baring my soul to."

Well, now she knew where she stood. The dancing-with category. She was here as part of her dance tutoring. Though she didn't get how what they were doing right now would help.

"My brother was killed for the small amount of money he had on him. Marguerite adopted only me."

She went completely still as she waited for him to continue, hoped for his sake he would. *If* he was going to continue. How her heart hurt for that poor little boy, his mother and his brother.

A muscle twitched in his jaw. "I was ten and scared to death."

Oh good lord, no kidding. She'd been on her own at eighteen and scared to death. And she had a home to go to and people to help her. He was ten and lost everything. She frantically blinked to get rid of the tears that filled her eyes. He was so tense she thought he might break if she so much as breathed. He wiggled the fingers on his bandaged hand, and she wondered if he itched to make a fist with them. When he started to speak again, some of the tension left him, though he kept his eyes on the darkening horizon.

"Marguerite was a retired professional dancer turned instructor and she owned a theater. She took me in, eventually adopted me and gave me everything I have. She taught me to dance professionally, educated me and left me all she owned when she died. If it wasn't for her, I'd probably be dead myself." He pulled a chain that hung around his neck out from under his t-shirt and a wedding ring dangled from it. "This is hers. Her husband died before I knew her, and she never took it off her finger until she gave it to me the day she died. She told me to give it to the woman I want to marry. Since I have no intention of ever getting married, I wear it around my neck as a tribute to her."

Jade relaxed as her heart returned to a more normal

rhythm, and she took a sip of her wine. "She had no family?"

"No."

"So you both needed someone to love and to love you."

He jumped to his feet with a derisive snort and walked a few paces away, his hands clasped behind him. His rigid back was towards her, and she felt like he'd done it deliberately.

"I don't do love, *chica.*" He turned then. "I don't do…" He waved his hand around. "*This.*"

She stood, not liking the way he towered over her, and set her wineglass on a nearby table. She narrowed her eyes for a moment, then raised her eyebrows. "This?"

He waved his hand around again. "This—how do you say?—sharing confidences? Lesson over. I have some things I need to take care of now." He shoved his good hand in his pocket. "Normally I would have you practice what we've gone over at home and come back in a week. With your—situation—I think you need to come back in three days. Is that doable for you?"

She forced herself to act normal, to pretend she didn't care the evening was over and he'd suddenly put a barrier between them, but mostly that she didn't care it was all part of her *lesson.* He hadn't shared his past for any other reason than to gain her trust. Although his reaction had her wondering if it had something to do with the 'L' word.

"I'm not sure. I have to check my calendar. I'll text you and let you know what works for me."

"The same time as today, possibly?"

She shrugged. She didn't want to appear eager to

schedule a time with him—or available whenever he wanted. So she was glad her life was busy and her reason for not complying to his demands true. "I'm not sure. Hopefully we can coordinate something on such short notice. I have a dress fitting with Lexi I need to work in as well." She pulled her keys from her pocket and dangled the ring on her finger.

He stepped toward her and she stiffened, not wanting him to touch her when he was in this weird mood. He narrowed his eyes at the action, but he merely walked by her and held the door to the house open. "I'll walk you to your car."

She nodded and went inside, hoping she came across as unconcerned while she headed to the front door. Which was difficult with him following close enough for her to feel his heat. She barely kept from jumping when he spoke.

"Whatever time works for you, I will make sure works for me."

Who was *this* guy, and what the heck happened to Han? "Did you tell me those things about yourself so I would trust you?"

His eyes went from hard topaz to fiery yellow momentarily before hardening again. He gave a slight nod. "*Si.* I think we made some progress today. I don't want to slide backwards, so we will be spending more time together off the dance floor as well as on."

****

In an effort to convince himself being with Jade didn't make him think about things he shouldn't be thinking about, or wanting things he knew he *didn't* want, he stuffed the desire to slam the door behind him and closed it with soft deliberation instead. He knew what his issue was. He was so busy getting his dance studios going, it had been a while since he'd enjoyed the company of a woman. He'd call one of his lady friends to see if she was up for a good time tonight, let off some steam, and everything would be back to normal.

He was getting way too stuck in a track called Jade, but it was merely the challenge of her, that was all. And the fact she was so different from the women he usually enjoyed. And that she wasn't trying to get his attention. And how sarcastic and spunky she was. And brave. He let out a string of colorful words in Spanish. Even when she wasn't here, she was invading his life.

He pulled his cell phone out of his pocket and scrolled through his contacts. Who would be fun to hang out with tonight?

Four hours later he let himself back in his house, and this time he slammed the door behind him. He ended up at party thrown by a friend he worked with on *Celebrity Dance,* believing it would be the perfect solution to his problem. Plenty of women, plenty of whatever might take his fancy, distractions galore. Unfortunately, the only difference between now and the time when Jade left was his blood alcohol level. Well, his bad mood had escalated too. He couldn't decide who he was more ticked off at, himself or Jade. Because of her, his usual blow-off-steam, have-some-fun tactics didn't work like they usually did. And he still needed a cold shower. None of the women vying for his attention held any appeal. Hadn't even turned him on the way merely thinking about Jade did. He was so screwed. And so angry about it he wanted to break something.

He let out a growl of frustration and started tearing off his clothes as he headed across his bedroom to the en suite bathroom. He was desperate enough to see if a cold shower would solve the problem with his brain as well as his libido, and grateful he could afford to pay someone to pick up after him. The way he felt right now, those clothes could stay on the floor and rot. He had the same opinion about the splint on his arm, but that he put on the counter in the bathroom. He couldn't afford to damage his arm any further. Thankfully only another week and he'd be done with that.

He turned on the shower, adjusted the temperature to as cold as he could stand and stepped under it, sucking in his breath when the cold stream hit him. After taking a moment to get acclimatized, he grabbed the soap and started cleaning off the last remnants of the evening.

And his mind went right back to Jade like a broken record. One measly dance lesson and she'd infected his brain. Why couldn't he stop thinking about her? At first, it was only her gorgeous legs. *De nada*. She wasn't the first woman to plant those sort of visions in his head. Though he had to admit, he'd be hard-pressed to remember anyone else with legs as riveting as hers...

It didn't take long to go from thinking about the physical to thinking about the person. Long before she arrived for her first lesson, he missed matching wits with her. Had looked forward to what she'd dish out to him. Much less the opportunity to admire her legs— with his eyes *and* hands.

He knew things were going to get emotional for her. That there would be issues he needed to help her cope with. He'd been dealing with that aspect of his career since Marguerite had taken him in. He'd seen it; he'd helped others through it. Hell, he'd even done a little emotional exorcising of his own. He put his past behind him with no intention of thinking about it again. Buried so deep he was confident nothing could make it resurface. He never told *anyone* what his mother did for a living. The only ones who knew anything were Marguerite and Beck, and that was bare bones. He was perfectly content with that part of his life buried in the past. Thriving, actually. Until her.

Though his brain wasn't frozen into compliance, other parts of him were, so he viciously turned off the water and stepped out of the shower. He jerked a towel off the rack and dried himself with it as he headed to the bedroom. When he threw himself on the bed, not bothering to pull back the covers, Flamenco gave a yowl of complaint and jumped off it, slinking away with a dirty look.

"Ah, *gatito*, I'm sorry to scare you away. You sense my mood and know it's time to hide, don't you?"

****

"I'm so sorry I'm late. It looks like you gave up and started without me."

Jade nodded and tried to hide her irritation. Tardiness was a habit she hadn't been able to break Lexi of. "The seamstress has a schedule to keep, and I didn't want to put her behind. What do you think of the dress?"

"Hey, you don't need to use your mom voice anymore; we're both adults." Lexi's eyes narrowed as she looked Jade over. She walked around the circular platform where Jade stood to view the dress from all sides. She rubbed the lilac silk between her fingers and when she sighed, Jade's stomach dropped. "Geez, I don't know. It seemed so perfect the first time you tried it on."

"You wouldn't shut up about it. You don't seriously think it's no good now."

"I'm just not feeling it today, Jay-Jay. Besides, when we picked it out, we weren't planning on your dancing in it."

The seamstress stopped fiddling with the dress and stepped back when Jade growled, "Lexi."

"Don't you start. You said you want me to have the perfect wedding."

Jade bit back the words that rose in her throat. So they were going down this road today.

"I do, I really do. And I think this dress is perfect. It's the color and style you want, and it's comfortable and flattering, so I like it. What more do you need?"

"A fuller, shorter skirt and a color that doesn't wash you out. That lilac shade is too pale."

"Excuse me." Jade and Lexi looked at the seamstress. "Would you like me to get a salesperson to help you find a different dress? She can also let you know how long it will take to order it."

They spoke at the same time.

"No."

"Yes."

"Lexi, please. This dress is wonderful; the color is the exact one you picked for the wedding. Now, if it was your dress, I could see changing your mind because you're the center of attention, but mine isn't that important. Let's stick with this one and save everyone's time."

"You want me to ask Han what he thinks about

your dancing in this?"

Jade rubbed her temples; the classical music playing over the speakers of the shop suddenly seemed unbearably loud. "Lord no. Don't involve Han in this." She wasn't prepared to deal with him yet. She was still emotionally reeling from her dance lesson's unexpected turn.

Too late. Lexi had snapped a picture with her phone and texted him. "Done."

What were the odds he didn't have his phone with him? Lexi's text alert went off. Looked like zero.

"He says you look *lo*…Geez, it's in Spanish." She walked over and showed her the text. "Do you know what that means?"

"Um…" *Good enough to eat.* No way in hell would she translate that for her little sister. Even if she was an adult on the verge of getting married.

Lexi laughed. "I bet it's something sexy. If I wasn't so in love with Beck, I'd probably melt at Han's feet. For you, the blush is a good sign. Does he know you speak fluent Spanish?"

She lifted one shoulder and suppressed a twinge of guilt as she recalled his muttered prayer in the elevator. "I'm not sure. Doesn't matter anyway. The rest of his text is in English and says, plain as day, it won't work."

"Told you. Time to go shopping."

Jade groaned. How many dresses would she have to try on this time? She hated clothes shopping. "Needs must, I suppose."

"I wonder if Han can help us pick something out."

As much as she'd enjoy seeing Han—which she was loathe to admit, even to herself—the idea of him watching her try on dresses freaked her out. "You do that and I will not only quit the dance lessons, I'll quit the wedding."

Lexi laughed again. "Me thinks Han may be more than you can handle. And I have yet to see anything you can't handle. If I didn't think it would affect my wedding, I'd tell him to get over here and help us." She shook her head. "Hurry up and get back in your own clothes so we can start looking."

A customer squeaked some hangers along a rack and Jade cringed. The idea of looking through a bunch of dresses again was daunting. "Lexi, I'm no good at that kind of stuff. Can't I just sit here and wait while you find some for me to try on?"

"I like having you with me to bounce ideas off. Plus, maybe you'll learn something along the way that will help you pick better clothes for yourself."

"I don't care about that. Business clothes for the office and comfortable things for home. I'm all set." She briefly closed her eyes. "I'm going to need a glass of champagne."

Lexi chuckled. "I'll let the proprietor know. I'm surprised you didn't ask for one the minute you walked in here like you did last time when we picked out your dress." She scowled. "Come with me, Jay-Jay, or I'm going to nominate you for that show…What's it called again?"

Jade kept her mouth shut. She knew exactly which show that was. She'd been sucked into it for one season. It hadn't helped her pick out clothes or given her a desire to do so.

Lexi snapped her fingers. "*What Not to Wear.*"

"It's off the air, so your threat is no good." Jade sighed and stepped off the platform. Another battle lost.

Had she given in to her so often Lexi had her wrapped around her finger? Tears and slamming doors echoed through her mind. No, she'd just gotten tired of the fight by the time Lexi went to college. Plus, it was her *wedding.* She was allowed to change her mind as many times as she wanted. "You win. Back in a minute."

Half an hour later, her glass of champagne was empty, and the changing room was filled with a dozen dresses for her to try on, a few in varying shades of purple. The rest fit the lesser colors Lexi chose for her wedding. Grabbing one at random, she put it on, not an easy task because of the cut of the dress, which was another reason she picked her clothes for comfort rather than style, and headed out of the dressing room to parade before Lexi and the saleswoman.

"This one looks good; how about we go with it?"

The dress fit well—meaning it didn't hang like a sack. The full skirt hit just below the knees. With her height, they usually hit a lot higher up the thigh. Another reason she owned only one dress. The black one which Han hated. *Used to own.*

"*Horrible!* And before you waste any more time trying things on that won't work, I want to have a look at the rest of the dresses you picked out."

Han. She might kill her sister before the wedding even took place. She took in a deep breath, tried to relax her shoulders and prayed anger hadn't turned her face red.

"I swear Jay-Jay, I didn't ask him to come. He just showed up a few minutes ago."

"Then how did he know where we were?"

Lexi bit her lip and looked down at her hands for a moment. "I may have told him."

"So you did—"

"No. I didn't."

"*Chicas*, stop bickering. When I asked Lexi what bridal shop you were at, she didn't know I intended to come. Now, can we get on with what we're here to do?"

Lexi put a hand on his arm. "Han, you really didn't have to come. I feel bad, taking up your time like this. You've already done enough with the dance lessons. I do know what I'm doing when it comes to fashion."

"I don't doubt that for a minute, Lexi, but there's more involved here than picking out a bridesmaid's dress."

Jade ground her teeth. "Just because you're in the wedding doesn't mean you can dictate to Lexi what dress to choose. What makes you think it's okay to come here uninvited and take over?"

She bit her lip. It was not her intention to make things worse for Lexi, but the thought of Han looking her over in each dress made her squirm. And something else she couldn't put her finger on. Han's hot gaze raked her face. Was it anger or passion? Jade wasn't sure which one would be better, but she did know the tingling sensation it lit inside her was something she didn't want.

He relaxed his stance and sighed. "*Chica,* it wasn't my intent to upset Lexi, or you, but you need to remember that a celebrity is part of this wedding, which changes things more than you may realize. For myself, Han, I don't care what dress you choose. Lexi, you have good judgment, and as long as Jade can dance comfortably, I'm good. For Alejandro Rivera, this is a different thing. People will only look at the celebrity, not the friend. Judgments will be made about what I am wearing, what my partner is wearing, and how well I was able to teach Jade to dance. The media will be there to take pictures and write up a story—"

"Oh hell, no! Lexi's wedding is not going to be some publicity stunt for you. Is that why you offered the free dance lessons?"

Han swiped a hand down his face. "I'm guessing Lexi didn't tell you."

"Jade, it's okay. Beck and I have already talked about this with Han, the day after he offered the lessons." She placed a hand on Jade's arm. "It will be an exclusive story, to one magazine, and they will only be at the reception to cover the dancing."

Jade lifted an eyebrow, wishing her champagne glass wasn't empty. "Well, that's a relief…"

Lexi nodded and continued, "By offering the exclusive, the wedding won't become a media event once the public knows Han is involved, and he'll have some security there in addition to the security provided by Greystone Manor. It's part of the territory with being a celebrity and we realized, when Beck decided to ask Han to be the best man, there would be some kind of media circus over it, before the dancing even became part of it."

Jade looked up at the ceiling for a moment. She was not going to explode. She was *not*. If Lexi was okay with all the insanity surrounding Alejandro Rivera, she needed to be, too. Still, it would have been nice if someone had clued her in before now.

"So, that being the case, it's my reputation on the line here. On top of which, I have experience with this kind of thing. I've picked out dance costumes since I was a teenager. Part of my job on *Celebrity Dance* is designing outfits for the dance numbers I choreograph." He stopped, glanced around the nearly empty store, a look of relief on his face as he glanced at his watch. "Can we get back to what we're here for?"

****

What started out as a simple, half-hour fitting turned into an afternoon marathon of trying on an endless parade of gowns, only to end up squirming beneath Han's critical gaze. The color was too dark or too light. The sleeves were too puffy or too long. The skirt was too straight or too full. As far as Jade was concerned *they* were being *too* picky.

She saved the current number for last, mainly because it was strapless and she didn't have the chest to hold it up. Other than that, once she put the dress on, she felt like it could be the one. It was the right colors for the wedding; the bright purple and celery-green chiffon made her eyes glow. The different colors of fabric crisscrossed around the bodice, then blended into a full, mid-calf skirt. Crystal rhinestones, laid out in a swirling floral pattern at the waist, were more bling than she'd ever wear, but they emphasized her small waist and highlighted curves she never realized she had. If only she filled out the top a little better…

Hand splayed across her chest to keep the dress from falling down or gaping open, she left the dressing room, praying Han hadn't found something else for her to try on. The look in Han's eyes when she came out of the dressing area sent sparks zinging down her spine. She lowered her lashes and couldn't bring herself to look at him again.

"I hope this is the one, because I really need to get

something to eat. It's got to be dinner time by now."
Jade's stomach growled. Even if it wasn't dinner time,
she needed food. "Although I'm not too sure about the
dress staying up, ever, never mind while I'm dancing.
Some kind of miracle will have to be performed."

Lexi giggled. "Seamstresses can do all kinds of
amazing things. I think the dress is perfect if the top can
be fixed. What do you think, Han?"

He walked towards her and her stomach flipped.
Several more times too by the time he reached her. He
was going to touch her and she had to act normal. She
still had no clue what that was with him. Taking her
hand, he helped her step down off the platform and led
her to one of the many mirrors in the room. After
positioning her in front of it, he stepped behind her. It
wasn't a new sight. She'd seen reflections of them close
together during their dance lessons. So why did it get
her all flustered now?

"Hmmm...I do like it."

Without warning, he took the back of the bodice in
his good hand and pulled it tight across her chest. As
his eyes perused the picture she made in the mirror, the
look in them changed from critical to satisfied. He bent
his head a fraction and whispered, "*Si, chica.* In this
dress, you look good enough to eat for dinner and
dessert. Tailored to the right size, it will show your
figure in all its glory. It may even make Beck think he
picked the wrong sister."

In the mirror's reflection, she saw the color rush to
her cheeks and resisted the urge to cover them with her
hands. The heat of his body enveloped her from behind;
the merest touch of a knuckle against her bare skin
made her go weak in the knees. She fought the desire to

lean back against him. When he ran a finger down her hot cheek and rested the hand on her shoulder, she nearly sighed in ecstasy.

It didn't bode well for the near future, and she didn't like the physical power he had over her. How could he make her melt with the mere touch of his hands and his breath in her ear? Watching him in the mirror as he whispered in her ear had been a bad idea. It was the sexiest picture she'd ever seen. The fact she was part of that picture made it even more so.

"I doubt that. So, is this the one?" She forced her gaze from the reflection of her and Han to Lexi. "What do you think?"

"I think that I wish I'd been the one to pick out that dress. It's perfect. Rather, once it's tailored, it'll be perfect. I'll go get a seamstress to take your measurements and set up a time for another fitting."

Jade nearly sagged with relief. If it hadn't meant she'd end up leaning against Han, she would have. "Okay, I agree with both of you that this dress looks great."

"Oh my God, I believe in miracles. Jade actually *likes* a dress. Han, I am seriously impressed with your skills."

Jade held up a hand. "Whoa, there. Just because it looks like a dream doesn't mean I'm happy with it. Can you guarantee the thing won't fall down while I'm dancing in front of a room full of people and the *media?*"

Han nodded, and she felt his hair brush hers with the movement. He really was too close, but she couldn't muster up the desire to make him move. Besides, he was holding up her dress.

"This I will promise," he said, his voice deeper and his accent thicker than usual. "If the seamstress here can't do it, then I will take it to the costume department at *Celebrity Dance* and have them take care of things."

Jade's shoulders relaxed. "Okay then. Thank God that's over. Lexi, you're treating me to dinner at our favorite Mexican place. I need *food*. It's been a very taxing afternoon."

Han raised his brows. "I hope it's because of trying on all those dresses and not because of me."

"No comment."

Chapter Eight

"You want me to *what?*"

They were waist-deep in the ocean that was Han's backyard when he announced he wanted to try a lift. Why didn't he say anything before she put on a swimsuit and waded into the water?

"You're going to put a *lift* in our routine? This isn't a dance competition, Han, it's a wedding, for crying out loud. There's no need for theatrics."

He chuckled and gave her a wicked smile. "It's a trust exercise, *chica;* there will be no lifts in the dance. Unless you want to do it…"

"Good lord, *no.*" She wiped a stray lock of hair off her face and shook her head. "I trust you. I simply don't see the need to jump in your arms and be lifted over your head to prove it."

His expression changed to serious. "This is where you're wrong. Now, back up a little more, come at me and jump. I will catch you and lift you up. If it goes awry, the worst that can happen is we fall in the water."

"Yeah, well, this water is really cold. Is there a nice warm pool we can do this in?"

"Take my word for it, the cold water is in your best interests."

She shrugged a shoulder and blew out a breath. He was right. Somewhat. If she didn't do it properly, they'd fall in the water, no worse for wear. But it didn't feel like falling was the worst that could happen. Reluctantly she nodded her head and backed away from him a bit, silently chanting, *for Lexi, for Lexi.* She would be moving with the waves, so it helped her momentum, but that meant Han had to brace himself against the water coming at him, as well as the impact of her, and she wasn't too sure he could do it. And the last thing she wanted to do was injure his wrist right after it'd healed.

"Han, I'm not a small person; I'm almost as tall as you and by no means a lightweight like you're used to dancing with. Are you sure you can do this?"

He chuckled. "*Chica*, do you doubt my strength? It seems this exercise is exactly what you need. It's a matter of timing and balance. When I position you at the right angle and hold you in the right spot, the effort it takes is minimized. The trick is getting that right and, like you say, I'm not used to doing it with someone built like you. Also, you have not done this sort of thing before, so you need to learn the procedure, and the water makes it easier. Are you afraid of falling in and getting your head wet?"

She snorted derisively. "Of course not. I've been playing in the ocean most of my life. If you think you can handle me, then let's do this."

Just in case, she mentally prepared herself to end up in the water. It was stupid. If this was no big thing, why was her heart pounding so hard? Han was her teacher and she was learning a dance move. Granted, it was a lift and he would be holding her up in the air, but still…She closed her eyes, took a deep breath and didn't open them until after she started moving.

Her timing was way off, and she misjudged how

hard it would be to jump out of the water, so she didn't get near high enough. Her hands latched onto his shoulders as she slammed against him. The water splashed around them, landing on her face and arms. He grabbed her by the hips to lift her but ended up merely steadying her. He didn't come close to losing his balance in the water, though he did suck in a breath between his teeth. Other than that, the impact on him was minimal. It reminded her of his reaction when the elevator came to a jarring halt.

It gave her some confidence in his ability to hold up his end of the lift. However, the feel of his slick, wet, *naked* flesh under her hands and along the length of her body was altogether a different story. She'd been scared of feeling a man's skin touching hers—afraid she might freak out like when she felt her stepfather's bare skin. Worse, afraid she would never enjoy it the way most women did.

Therefore, she wasn't prepared for how good it felt. Or that she wouldn't want to end to it. She resisted the urge to run her hands down his biceps, to press her lips to his and taste the salt of the ocean

How many times on his TV show had she watched the professionals practicing this very move with their students? As if it was part of an exercise routine, a maneuver they repeated until they got it right, with nothing remotely sexual about it. She hoped none of what was going through her head showed on her face as she removed her hands and stepped back a pace. Only when she wasn't pressed against him did she think about how her barreling into him may have affected him.

"Did I hurt you?"

He let out a throaty laugh. "It takes more than that to knock me off my feet, *chica*. It'll take a few tries for you to get a sense of how to do it in the water. Go again."

"That sounds like a challenge."

****

The cold water had him fantasizing about, and looking at, parts of her he shouldn't be thinking about. At all. Was he ever wrong thinking the coldness would keep his body from responding to her proximity. And those legs. *Ai ai ai!* Wrapping around him in an effort to keep them from falling over. Tangling with his when they toppled into the water. He found himself touching them way more often than he should for his own peace of mind. And, she didn't flinch at his touch once. Although, the way he felt right now, he *wished* her issues would surface so she'd call a halt to this torture. She bounced into him and slid down him more often than not.

They unbalanced several times as he tried to lift her. It was a long time since he'd lifted someone as tall as she was, and falling backwards into the ocean with her landing on top of him, the odds were increasing she'd realize her effect on him. One step forward and two steps back was not the purpose of the exercise. His normal male reaction to her was something she didn't have a normal experience with, and the thought of engendering feelings in her remotely like the ones her stepfather had, made him cringe.

He started this escapade hoping for one good lift to show her how far she could trust him. That he could hold her over his head and she was safe. Doing it at his private section of the beach rather than a public pool gave them the privacy they needed. He also hoped it would make her more comfortable with his nearness. He decided she'd made good progress with the comfortable aspect, it was time to give up on the lift aspect before he undid the good he'd already accomplished. At the moment, he could barely think past his desire to haul her into his house so she could wrap those legs around him in a way that would be exquisitely satisfying. For both of them. The heat of the morning sun on his back was nothing compared to the inferno raging inside him.

He grabbed her hand and helped her to her feet, then slicked his wet hair back off his forehead with his hand. "Okay, we're done. I don't need to trash my wrist right after it's healed…"

His voice petered away as he looked into her eyes, and it wasn't fear he saw. Was she as affected as him from their tangling in the surf? He stepped closer, resting his hands on her bare shoulders. *Just a kiss*. They'd already kissed and she hadn't freaked out. Hell, he'd pressed her up against the wall of the elevator and kissed her like he never wanted to stop, and she kissed him right back. His blood throbbed through his veins at the thought, the need to press himself against her increasing. The cool ocean breeze across his wet skin didn't cool him a bit. His voice was hoarse when he spoke. "Jade?"

He slid an arm down across her back and pulled her close. Wrapping his other hand around the back of her neck, he tipped her face towards him with a thumb under her jaw. He lowered his head and softly rubbed his lips against hers, taking it slow for fear she might bolt. Or punch him or kick him. Or bite him. He suppressed a groan at the thought.

She relaxed into him, moving her mouth against his, and his heart pounded like a jackhammer trying to tear its way through his chest. He ached to pull her tightly into his arms, to rub himself against her, to immerse himself in her. Something he dare not do. For his sake even more than hers. How stupid of him to think one kiss would solve anything. So he ended it, easing away from her to place his hands on her shoulders for a moment before he let her go and stepped back.

"That was totally out of line." He cleared his throat. "As much as we both enjoyed it, it's not a good idea to get involved sexually while we're working on the dance for the wedding. I said I wouldn't get physical with you, so I apologize."

He paused, eyes searching hers. There was no fear, which made his heart take wing for a moment before it pounded hard at the regret he saw there. "From here on out, I'm thinking it's a good idea to stay away from the water and keep our clothes on." He shook his head at himself. "This was an epically bad idea. I don't know why I thought it would work. Your legs are lethal weapons, and not only seeing the length of them in that swimming suit but having them wrapping around me and tangling with mine in the water is—a bit distracting. I pride myself on my self-control." He ran a hand around the back of his neck, massaging the tight muscles for a moment. At least it had kicked in before he picked her up and took her to his bedroom. He sighed. "Let's get dressed. Time to try something different."

She shuffled a foot in the sand for a moment,

watching it like it was the most fascinating thing she'd ever seen. "You really like my legs?" she said softly, then cleared her throat. "Something different?"

She raised smoldering green eyes to his, and a hot flame of desire hit him in the gut before quickly spreading outward. He was thrilled with the fact he was the one to awaken a desire for physical contact in her. And it wasn't the usual thrill he got when he set out to capture the interest of a woman he was attracted to. It was more than sexual. He put the brakes on that train of thought. He didn't want to know what else it meant. He was giving a dance lesson. Not the sort he usually gave, but a lesson regardless. He needed to get his head where it belonged.

"We're going to do the rest of our lesson at Let's Dance."

"Whoa. I'm not taking my car into East L.A. by myself, much less parking it. There'll be nothing left of it come time for me to leave. Unless I can park it in your Fort Knox of a garage."

He lifted a brow. "No kidding. I'll follow you to your house and we'll drop off your car, then you can ride with me."

****

Han followed her to her house in an old pick-up, but as Jade climbed in, she couldn't relax and enjoy the ride. The thought of dancing in a class full of people tied her up in knots. Tighter than the ones she got when she thought about dancing at the wedding.

As he pulled away from the curb, she looked over at him. "How many cars do you own? And why a beat up old truck?"

"Three. You've seen them all now. It's always

handy to have a truck and this is the first vehicle I ever owned. But besides the sentimental value, it makes me feel like a show-off taking a fancy car to Let's Dance. I want the kids to relate to me, not to feel like they're less-than. That I'm some god-like person living a life they can never have. But for chance, their life would've been mine."

She swallowed. How could you not admire a celebrity who didn't forget where he came from, much less one who wanted to do what he could to help others get where he was? Or at least have a better life? Still, it didn't mean she was any more comfortable with having her dance lesson around other people.

"It makes no sense to me how this latest escapade is going to help with my dancing. Or is it that you have to be at Let's Dance, so you're killing two birds with one stone?"

He gave her a mischievous smile, then turned his attention back to the road. Her heart acknowledged it with a vicious thump. Had she ever seen a better looking man? Stupid question. This was L.A. Of course she'd seen better looking men. She had an actor-wannabe as a client who was seriously swoon-worthy. She squeezed her eyes shut in an effort to block the thought that suddenly popped in her head. Was it other things, things she'd learned about him since spending time with him, things about the man inside that made him more attractive? *No.* She wasn't that stupid. Getting emotionally involved with a celebrity was absolutely idiotic.

"I have a class to teach in half an hour, so, the two birds thing."

Yeah. Definitely not the man making him more

attractive. Right now, she could happily strangle him. If he wasn't driving the car she was riding in, that was. "Maybe you should turn around and take me home. I don't think I'm up for making a fool of myself in front of a group of teenagers. Never mind underprivileged ones with issues."

He didn't slow down the car and he didn't look at her, but his jaw clenched. Worse than that? She'd not only irritated him but said something she wished she hadn't as soon as the words were out of her mouth. Yet *still* her fingers itched to push a stray lock of hair off his forehead. A desire which freaked her out more than the puzzle of his attraction. She was suppressing the urge *to* touch someone, not the urge to back away. The feelings she'd had in the elevator weren't a fluke due to their unusual circumstance. Suddenly she felt as though she couldn't breathe. It was absolutely the worst time to realize the extent of his power over her, because the fact Han was taking her to have a lesson with a group of people was more than enough to make her feel like she was suffocating.

"I can see I'm helping you with another kind of trust as well. You need to trust my judgment. And be careful, your prejudice is showing."

For the first time since she'd heard it, the sound of his voice didn't make her want to melt; it chilled her to the bone.

"Han—"

"No, Jade, I do not want to hear it."

His accent was thicker and as he viciously shifted gears, she fought the sudden urge to throw up. Prudently she kept her mouth shut. Because he was right. And she didn't want to be that person. She wasn't that person. She was, however, seriously freaked out about what he wanted her to do. Which meant she had no choice but to trust his judgment. Although she really didn't get how making her take part in the class was going to help. Private lessons were hard enough. If her dance partner was anyone other than him, she wouldn't be the only one thinking this was a bad idea.

She watched the city go by in silence, refusing to look anywhere but out her window and tried to think about anything but Han and dancing.

"Did I really just see a building shaped like a green tamale?"

He cracked a smile and Jade mentally sighed with relief. "You did. It's a beauty salon now, but it was a tamale place back in the day."

She chuckled. "Classic. Love that about L.A."

"The dance studio used to be a tortilla factory. Take a good look at the reception desk. It's an old tortilla-making machine. I had a granite top put on it so it could function as a desk. I found the machine in a room where the previous owner stashed a bunch of junk. Most everything else got thrown away, but I kept the tortilla maker as a tribute to the history of the building."

"I can't believe I didn't notice before. I love how you did that."

"It's a little reminder for the kids of their heritage."

She swallowed a lump in her throat and prayed her voice sounded normal. "You're just what those kids need. The money you're spending on them and the time you're giving them. This isn't merely a tax write-off for you."

He gave a slight shake to his head and his hand

tightened on the gear shift, but he didn't look at her. Did he not *want* to look at her now? "There's the pay-it-forward aspect of it, but it's more than that. I *know* how hopeless these kids feel."

"And they can relate to you because of it, I bet. Do kids show up just to hang out with a celebrity?"

"It's happened, but generally I'm there when the studio is only open to kids who are serious about dancing. Not necessarily good at it but have a real desire to do it. I have security guards to keep things under control, and I'm usually not there when it's open to whoever wants to show up."

He darted a glance at her, his eyes cold and hard as topaz. She suppressed a shiver and fondled her locket for a moment. She'd touched a nerve and had no idea what to say or do to make up for it. He was sensitive and protective about the kids at Let's Dance. Which, in reality, made her admire him even more. She kicked herself for her inadvertent criticism, and she hated that it made him withdraw from her. She also hated how much she hated it. She wasn't sure what to do about it all either. Why did relationships with people have to be so complicated? Things were much easier when she spent most of her time living as a hermit playing with numbers.

"The class we're joining is a special one I've started. It's only open to those who put forth the effort to try out for it and qualified with both skill and talent. I have no idea what you did, but you got through to Cat, and she wanted to be part of this. I really appreciate it."

And still, he didn't look at her. His hand had a death-grip on the gear shift and his voice lacked warmth. Not that she doubted the sincerity of what he told her.

"I was happy to do it, though I'm not sure what it was I did. I'm glad she's joined in." She looked down at her lap. Fiddled with the hem of her t-shirt. How was she going to handle joining a group of strangers without his moral support? "Han, I'm genuinely sorry about what I said. I didn't mean it to come across the way it did. I'm freaking out about doing this."

He nodded his head, his eyes on the road as he maneuvered the car into the garage at Let's Dance. "You'll be fine."

She didn't think so, but it didn't make much difference at this point, and all too soon for her peace of mind she was standing in a dance studio filled with about twenty teenagers. Surprisingly, the girls only outnumbered the boys by two. Which wasn't a problem as two other professional dance teachers were there, volunteering their time so everyone was able to pair up.

Dancing with an angry Han had her shaking in her shoes as she stood at the side of the room—probably more like cowered—not far from the door. She fought an urge to bolt through it and lock herself in his office. Especially when he announced they were going to be dancing the cha-cha-chá. As he explained what the class was about, she wondered why he wanted her there.

"I'm happy to see so many of you who not only have the talent but are willing to do the hard work necessary to pursue it. Before we begin, there's some things you need to know. First, though, I'd like you to meet my friend Jade. She's one of my students at Seriously Dance, but for reasons I won't go into, she's joining us for her lesson today. Be gentle with her, *por favor*."

There were a few chuckles and a couple of guys whistled. Not what she needed to get over her nerves, but it did make her feel accepted.

He clapped his hands together several times to restore order. "Now, the reason for this special class." He paused dramatically and everyone in the room was intently focused on him. Including her. "I'm putting on a dance program as a fundraiser, and I want this group to do a routine for it. People need to see the kind of talent we have here. What their money will be supporting. There will be performances by professionals from my dance show, as well as a dance number performed by my students at Seriously Dance."

This elicited cheers, groans and complaints, and he had to clap his hands again to get them to quiet down. When he started speaking, it was in Spanish. "I know this is rather overwhelming for some of you, as well as frightening, but I want all of you to give it a chance before you decide whether you want to take part or not. Then, if you don't feel up to it, you can quit. *But* you have to give it a try first. So, everyone is committed to doing this for a week. The fact you were willing to try out to be here in the first place tells me you're serious about your dancing. Don't let fear control you. Think instead of the possibilities open to you, the future you could have, which seemed unattainable not so long ago. There will be a number of high-powered entertainment people in attendance. A once-in-a-lifetime opportunity, so don't let fear keep you from grabbing it with both hands."

He switched back to English. "I know we usually do our classes in Spanish, but from now on we only use

English. Making a career of dancing in L.A. involves more than just memorizing routines and dance steps. I don't think this will pose much of a problem for most of you, but this is also part of your training."

Everyone was silent as they absorbed what he said and waited for him to continue. Jade was in awe of the respect he received, respect that went beyond the fact he was a celebrity. And what he was doing for these kids said volumes about him. As a man. As a person.

"Now the cha-cha. I am assigning who you're partnered with and you will be performing with them at the fundraiser. You're with this person because I feel it's the best match as far as talent, skill, personality and size. I put time and effort into this, so there will be no switching things around. Do not even go there. Since we have two extra girls, they will be paired with an instructor until I can find students to do it. Now, I'm going to put on some music, pair you up, and you can practice your cha-cha as well as get used to your new partner. While you're doing this, I'm going to show Jade the basics as it's all new to her."

Jade relaxed somewhat at the informality of it. Everyone was going to be busy with their own partners and, most likely, wouldn't be watching her stumble around. Still, she'd just as soon be home watching *Celebrity Dance* rather than having a dance lesson with one of its stars.

Han held his hand out to her as though it was a direct order. She placed hers in it and tried to concentrate on what he said. The dance started on the two with a count of eight. That was more of a foreign language to her than Spanish. She held up her free hand.

"Hang on a minute, there. I don't know dance lingo, and this is the first time we've used music in our lesson. Remember who you're working with here, Han."

He cracked a slight smile. "*Sí*. Sorry."

Cat yelled out, "I heard Spanish coming out of your mouth, *Señor* Alejandro!"

"Mind your own business, Cat. Do as I say, not as I do."

She flipped him off before doing as he ordered. Jade chuckled. It was nice to see the only thing about Cat that changed was her attitude about dancing. Watching her for a moment as she went back to doing the cha-cha, Jade realized she had some serious talent and hoped Han could help her to use it to better her life.

Han snapped his fingers in her face. "Focus Jade. Ignore the music. Watch me do the basic step, then mimic me. You start with your right foot, keep your knees soft—that means slightly bent—feet close to the ground. Foot stays in place for the first beat, then goes back on the second."

She really did try, but having her lesson here was a bad idea. In front of people. Doing the cha-cha. Watching *Alejandro Rivera* do the cha-cha. His fluid movements. The hip action. His long legs. A Latin dancing a Latin dance. Plus, he was so damn *hot*. Focus, coordination, relaxing into it. Impossible. As was trying to ignore the music. Disapproval emanated off him in waves that slapped at her, tossed her around and left her completely disoriented.

She wanted to go home. *Now*. Which was impossible. The icing on the cake? Han repeatedly barking out, *No, on the two* or *Concentrate* or *Feet close to the ground.* She didn't know if she wanted to cry or have a temper tantrum—or both. Her. Cool, calm, *uptight*, always-in-control Jade was on the verge of losing it.

There was a brief moment of relief when Han left her to have a conversation with one of the other instructors. Until said instructor came over to her when Han began to dance with his student. He held out a hand. "Hi, I'm Tristan."

She took it in a brief, strong handshake. Handshakes were part of her job. She could do those. As long as the person on the other end of it stayed outside her personal space bubble. "Jade."

His blue eyes twinkled at her and he struck her as a nice guy. How could he not? He was volunteering his time to help underprivileged children. "Lovely name. Goes with your eyes. Since Han needs to work with my student for a minute, I figured I'd help his. And since you seem to be having a hard time of it, I was thinking a change of partners might do the trick."

Before she realized his intention, he took her in dance hold and pulled her against him. "I know it probably feels weird, dancing with someone you don't know, but try to relax if you can. I'm not going to judge you; I'm here to help."

She stiffened instantly. Her heart pounded so hard, the blood started singing in her ears. She tried desperately to employ the relaxation techniques she'd perfected over the years. Was it like Tristan said, because she didn't know him and he was so close? It had been years since she'd felt this panicked. Realizing she wouldn't be able to conquer her reactions this time, she gulped in a breath and struggled free. At the perplexed look on Tristan's face she managed to form a few words. "No! I can't. I'm sorry."

She fled the studio, raced down the hall to Han's office and slammed the door behind her. She leaned against it and covered her face with her hands, her breath coming in gasps. She hated herself in that moment. Why couldn't she be like everyone else? Why did having a man hold her send her into a panic?

Much, much worse, The Devil of the Dance Floor, Alejandro Rivera, didn't produce the same reaction. She grabbed her locket in her fist and held on for dear life.

She'd made a complete fool of herself in front of a room full of teenagers. Much less Tristan, who'd done nothing wrong. Han was right. She could say no to Lexi. It wasn't the end of the world. There was a lot more to a marriage than having the perfect wedding day. Lexi would understand. She was still getting the perfect dance with Beck. It was enough.

She bit back a scream when the door started to move against her.

Chapter Nine

"Jade?"

The soft query in Han's voice made her melt. She moved away from the door, turning to face it warily as he entered and closed it behind him. "What happened?"

"Nothing," she said flatly. "Can you apologize to Tristan for me and take me home? Having my lesson here was also an epically bad idea."

Han took a few steps toward her but before he could say anything, Cat entered the room.

Jade barely stopped herself from swearing at her and telling her to get the hell out. She wanted to be home. Alone. But Cat started speaking before she could say anything. Which turned out to be a good thing because it kept her from making a fool of herself—again.

"I don't know what happened in there, but do I need to kick Tristan where it counts?"

With that, Cat did exactly what Jade needed. And she probably had no idea. Jade let out a breath and relaxed with it. Her mouth quirked up in a half-smile. "Not this time. I'll take a rain check though. Maybe you could tell him I'm sorry, but I'm not feeling well?"

She snorted derisively. "Whatever, Nerd. I'm not buying it, but maybe he will. Was kinda looking forward to some ass-kicking, but whatever." She paused and looked at her for a moment, then nodded her head once. "*Adios*."

Han looked at her silently while Cat left the room and closed the door behind her. "What happened?"

She crossed her arms and looked mutinously at him.

He blew out a frustrated breath. "Listen, *señorita*, you're the one who insisted on dancing in the wedding. I am willing to go the extra mile for this because Beck is like a brother to me, so whatever I need to do for you to make it happen, I'll do it. But you need to make up your mind and stop wasting my time if this is too much for you."

She turned away from him, rubbed the locket between her thumb and forefinger before she combed her hands through her hair. She couldn't think clearly when she looked at him. She got too caught up in the view.

What *did* she want? Could she do this or was she kidding herself because, deep down, what she actually wanted was to spend time with Han? And if that was her motive, she was well and truly screwed. She took a few deep, slow breaths in an effort to relax but it didn't work. Complicated thoughts and feelings swirled around inside her like a tornado. She couldn't latch onto anything that might ground her. Not even the locket did the trick this time.

"Right now, what I need is for you to leave me alone, Alejandro." At least she managed to get that out calmly and quietly, but she knew her tense shoulders and clenched hands told a different story. "I need a minute is all. Just—could you please go?"

She swore he growled in frustration before he closed the door behind him. She collapsed into a chair, but too agitated to stay there for long, she was back to pacing the room within moments.

She felt split in two and each half was having an almighty row with the other. She desperately wanted to move on from her past. To be around people without being ever-vigilant about getting too close. Most of the time it seemed like an impossible dream. But then there was Han, who could get close and her issues melted away. Maybe it wasn't so impossible after all. Then this. A perfectly normal guy, wanting no more than to help her learn some dance moves, and she was on the verge of a meltdown. If she'd never met Han, she'd be in the comfort zone of her little bubble right now, in blissful ignorance of the crazy emotions a single human being could arouse. A place where her issues for the most part no longer existed, and she lived a fairly satisfying life.

She stopped pacing. Her heart thundered in her chest as anger exploded and eclipsed everything else. Anger at her mother for dying and leaving her. Anger at her stepfather for coping with his loss in such a horrible way. And anger at herself for regressing when faced with the stress of getting close to a man. Anger at her therapist for telling her she wouldn't be completely healed until she faced her anger. But who was she *supposed* to be angry with?

The walls started closing in on her. She needed air. She needed space to move. She opened the office door and marched down the hall. She wanted out of here. Now. So badly she was stupidly oblivious to the fact she was a white girl in East L.A.

She headed down the sidewalk in a random direction, her shoes slapping the pavement so hard the noise echoed in her head. She sucked in air like she was suffocating and scrubbed away the tears that made it difficult to see. Stupid tears.

Why did her mother have to marry that disgusting, selfish man? Why did she have to die and leave Jade to pick up the pieces? To deal with raising Lexi alone, forcing Jade to grow up too soon. But worst of all, to be exposed to the lascivious desires of her stepfather. Damn *it*! She didn't want to have this hate and anger. It merely gave other people power over her. And until Han came along, she thought she was over it. Had all that time and money spent on therapy been a joke? *No.* She grabbed her locket, opened it and looked at the picture for a moment before closing it and letting it go. She knew there would always be times when there were too many stressors and she regressed. That was normal.

She was jerked back to reality when someone grabbed her arm and yanked it so hard her momentum spun her around to face them. Her personal space bubble was being invaded way too often of late.

Cat.

"Are you really that stupid?" Cat's gaze roamed her face, saw the tears. "Tristan *did* try to pull something. Or was it Han? Only a guy could get a girl crazy enough to make mistakes like the one you just did, coming out here by yourself."

"What?" Jade desperately tried to come to grips with the present and her eyes eventually focused on the view behind Cat. Trashed out cars abandoned on the side of the road, worn out old buildings covered with graffiti, corrugated metal fences topped with rings of barbed wire and painted with street art. "I guess I am stupid."

Cat let go of her arm and shook her head in disgust. "White chicks. Think they own the world and can do whatever they want."

"Not this one. I *wish* I could do whatever I want. And right now, that doesn't include going back to the studio. But it's the smart thing. Thanks for the wake-up call. I owe you one."

Cat shrugged a shoulder and the look in her eyes softened. She shook her hair back off her face. "Whatever. I'll hang with you if you want. I know what it's like to need to escape."

Jade hesitated. She didn't want to come across as ungrateful. It was a huge deal that Cat had offered to stay with her, even come after her for that matter. It sucked that what she wanted more than anything right now was to be alone.

Cat's eyes hardened as she snorted with disgust and stepped back a pace. "Never mind. I get it. Not the right type for you to be seen with. Even in my 'hood. What an idiot I am for thinking you were different."

"Good lord, Cat, not at all. The fact you came after me is enough to make me cry." Then, when Cat wrinkled her nose, she said, "Not that I will. I'm lame, but not that lame." Jade smiled faintly and looked at her for a moment before looking down at her hands. She was wringing them together and hadn't realized it. "The smart thing for me to do is go back to the studio, but what I really want is to be by myself. Outside. On a beach."

"*That* I can help you with. If you've got money or a bus pass."

"I do but it's in Han's car. Never mind. I guess I need to put on my big girl panties and go back."

"Well, you can't go anywhere alone here, that's for sure; you'll get killed or attacked, or worse, but I have an idea where you could go."

Jade raised her brows, the vice around her heart easing a bit. "Really?"

"*Señor* Alejandro's garage."

"It's locked."

"Yeah, but I have the key."

"He gave you the card key to his garage?"

"No. He has no idea. And if he finds out I have one, you're going to pay." Cat gave her a hard look then swore in Spanish. "What is it with you? You get me to do things I don't *want* to do."

Jade stiffened, and the look on her face made Cat laugh wickedly. "I have no clue. It surprises me as much as it does you."

"Whatever the hell it is, it works on *Señor* Alejandro too. He's…Hell, I don't know, *suave*— softer—around you."

"If you watched one of our dance lessons, I think you wouldn't feel that way."

"Whatever. Just keep your damn mouth shut."

Jade held up her hands. "Your secret's safe with me. But how did you get his key if he didn't give it to you, and how does he not know you have it?"

"What, you think because I've had a weak moment with you, I'm telling you all my secrets? Do you want to do this or not?"

"All right. Geez. You're as mercurial as Han. Anyway, if you can get in the garage, I have access to my purse. Which means I can catch a bus to Venice Beach."

They returned to the studio and went to the

underground garage without running into anyone except the receptionist at the front door. Cat pulled the card key from the pocket of her sweatpants, opened the door and walked in like she owned the place.

"You come here often?"

"Mmmm…Sometimes. Mostly when *Señor* Alejandro isn't here." She scrunched her nose. "When my mom has customers."

"Customers? She runs a business out of your house? Which I'm guessing you don't like."

"Technically. A cash business that gives her extra income."

"Han said she was an exotic dancer."

"That too, though she's going to have to give that up soon. Middle aged exotic dancers don't go over very well. Hell, you can't be that innocent and I know you're smart. Think about it."

"She sells herself."

Cat nodded and shrugged like it didn't matter, but the look on her face said she cared a lot. "She brings men home from the club for extra cash. So she can buy tequila."

No wonder Han had a soft spot for her and wanted to do everything he could to make her life better. "Does that make you angry with her?"

She shrugged again. "Thought this was about you and your meltdown, not me. My turn to give you the third degree."

Cat closed the garage door and stepped closer.

Han wasn't the only one who had a soft spot for Cat. And she could ask herself the same thing Cat had wondered about her. What was it with these two that drew her out of her shell? "Fire away."

"What's the deal with Tristan? *Did* he try to pull something?"

Jade crossed her arms and turned away from Cat, rubbing her biceps like she was suddenly cold. She'd never talked to anyone about her past other than her therapist and now, in the space of a few weeks, she'd not only told Han, she was on the verge of telling Cat. But this was a good thing, wasn't it? With Cat it might help Jade get closer to her, help her put her life on a different path so she could do better than her mother.

"It wasn't Tristan. I—have some issues. Because of something that happened when I was seventeen."

"Oh, you have *issues.* Poor little *gringa.* My mother is an exotic dancer and a whore. Get over yourself."

Jade clenched her teeth and turned back to face Cat. "My mother died when I was seventeen and my stepfather couldn't keep his hands off me. In order to protect my twelve-year-old sister, we moved out. I took care of her until she was old enough to be on her own."

Cat swore in Spanish. "I guess no one's immune from life taking a dump on them."

She dropped her hands and fisted them at her sides "Han is the first man to touch me who doesn't give me the creeps. And I'm pissed. I don't want to freak out when someone like Tristan gets too close."

"Are you mad at Han? He shouldn't have brought you here in the first place." She crossed her arms. "Maybe we should form a Men-Are-Jerks club."

Jade let out a little laugh, though laughing was the last thing she felt like doing. "That's the thing. Right now, I can't sort out my head enough to know who I'm mad at, why I'm mad, or even *what* I'm supposed to be feeling right now."

Cat raised her brows but didn't say anything. Jade raised her fists and pressed them into the sides of her head as though that might make the feelings go away, but it did nothing, so she dropped them.

"Who are you mad at, Nerd?"

"Damn it, I feel like I'm mad at my mother, but she didn't *do* anything wrong. Still, why did she have to marry that disgusting, selfish man? Why did she have to die and leave me to pick up the pieces? To deal with raising Lexi alone, forcing me to grow up too soon. She left me, Cat, to be mauled by my stepfather. It's not fair! And then I look at you and Han, and everything you've had to deal with, and I think I'm ridiculous for letting it bother me so much."

Cat crossed her arms and sighed. "This world sucks, and I've had a lot of experience with how this world can suck. It makes me angry, too. Sometimes really angry. That's another reason why I come here. It's better than doing something stupid that would make my life suck even more. Like be a gang whore. But that doesn't minimize what happened to you. Some people just have more crap dumped on them than others. Get mad at your mom or whoever else you feel mad at. You have the right to. There's stuff in here you can punch too, if you want. Hell, punch Han's truck for all I care. Sometimes you need to get it out in a way that doesn't make your life worse."

Tears sprang to her eyes, even slid down her cheeks. Angry tears, but in the anger was admiration for Cat's insight. She was tough. She had to be tough to get by in the neighborhood she lived in. But she was smart too.

"Damn it, Cat! I don't want to cry. It's stupid and doesn't fix anything. I know that for a fact. And punching Han's truck will hurt more than it will help."

"So scream, or whatever it is you need to do to get it out. I'll leave you alone so you won't feel so inhibited." She sighed. "I don't want Han to kick me out of the group, so I better go back for a bit at least. I'll let him know he needs to leave you alone to buy you some time. I'll get back here as soon as I can and if you still want to go to Venice Beach, I'll help you."

"Thanks, Cat. I owe you big time. Seriously. Come to me for anything, anytime. I'll give you my phone number and address."

Chapter Ten

Han knew he was at fault, but it took a while to get past the anger and figure out why he was upset. He didn't want to admit *he* was his own problem. Jade was nothing like the entitled, rich women he'd begged money from as a child, so as much as he wanted to lump her in with all the bad experiences in his past, he couldn't. But it was more than that. He hated this overpowering need to be in her company. And because of that desire, he'd made some bad decisions.

He shouldn't have brought her to Let's Dance. He knew she wasn't ready but convinced himself he could make it work. He had no business wanting a woman so badly he made stupid decisions. His mother made enough of those to last him a lifetime. If it was possible, he'd happily never see Jade again to avoid that pitfall. But it wasn't. So between his internal battle and getting Cat to tell him where Jade was, it was a couple hours before he knew where to find her. Which was someplace he rarely went because he risked being swarmed by fans. Hopefully he wouldn't need to be on the beach long.

She was easy to spot between her pale blond hair and the giant beach umbrella she sat under. He shoved his baseball hat into the back pocket of his jeans as he walked up to her and dropped down onto the sand next to her.

"You've made a loyal friend." He removed his sunglasses and set them down next to him. She didn't look at him, but didn't move away either, even though he'd purposefully invaded her personal space zone.

"Pretty full of yourself, aren't you?"

"You must be feeling better." His gaze roamed her profile, pausing a moment to admire her long, golden lashes. They were darker than her eyebrows, which were just shy of being white. He hadn't noticed that before. "I'm talking about Cat. I had a hell of a time getting her to tell me where you were. Though I think she meant to tell me all along. She was just stalling to give you time."

She glanced at him and then at the ocean. "Tell her thanks next time you see her."

"What's that supposed to mean?"

She shrugged a shoulder. "What you think it means. I'm not setting foot in Let's Dance ever again. As much as I like Cat."

"Slightly over-dramatic reaction, don't you think?" The same could be said for the way his gut twisted at the thought.

"No. And not for the reasons you think."

She didn't look at him, her attention absorbed by something on the ocean. His eyes followed the direction of her gaze, but he couldn't see anything worth looking at so intently.

"You have no idea what I'm thinking." God, he hoped that was true. Though half the time *he* didn't even know what he was thinking.

"You think I don't want to go back because I'm embarrassed."

Hell. What else had she figured out? "And it's not?

Or at least part of it?"

She shook her head and *still* she didn't look at him. "I'm through with all of it. Just trying to figure out how to break the news to Lexi."

His stomach sank. And not because he'd failed with a student for the first time in his life. Though technically it was the first time he'd taught someone for reasons other than because they wanted to improve their dance skills. Just thinking about it made him want to squirm. But that was just an ego thing. He'd learned early in his career to ignore his ego. Right now, he wished the problem *was* his ego. Egos, though fragile, were much simpler than what he was dealing with.

He looked over at her. For a long time. She truly was beautiful, not in the classic sense, not in the way that normally appealed to him. But in a way that compelled him nonetheless. And judging by the way he'd seen other men look at her, he wasn't the only one to feel that way. It consumed him now, the way it had that first night. Which forced him to acknowledge his attraction had nothing to do with a bad case of claustrophobia. *To hell with it!*

He took hold of her chin, not aggressively, but in a way that said he meant business, and captured her mouth. He'd been aching for it since this morning, and the intensity of his desire at the mere touch of her mouth made him gather her in his arms and push her back on the sand. Her instant response was his undoing. Common sense flew out the window. She was so sensual under that stiff, cool façade. Was it why she had such a strong reaction to what her stepfather had done?

The need to feel all of her more than he needed to dance overwhelmed him and he groaned from the depths of his being. He should've kissed her like this at the beach this morning, or the first night he brought her to his house. At least then they'd have the privacy needed to reach a satisfying conclusion. Still, knowing they were on a public beach didn't stop him. Not that he wasn't going to stop. He would. Soon. Just not yet. His thoughts spun away. All he could do was feel. Her. And it felt like he'd finally, after a lifetime, found his home. The place he wanted to be for the rest of his life.

No. Hell no!

He stiffened and scrambled to a sitting position. His heart thundered, and he raked his fingers through his hair. The thought wasn't enough to cool his desire but was enough to make him stop in his tracks. No woman was ever going to have that kind of power over him. He looked at her as she sat up next him, breathing heavily, and he shut his eyes to rid himself of the sight before it tempted him to doing something he absolutely should not do. A mere kiss and he felt ready to explode.

She blew out an exasperated breath and darted a look at him before returning her attention to the ocean. "Was that an attempt to change my mind, or something else?"

"I don't know what the hell that was. Momentary insanity?"

Suddenly restless, he looked around the beach. Apparently no one noticed them almost spontaneously combust. Thank goodness. He mentally shook his head. Only on Venice Beach.

She was silent for so long, he returned his attention to her. *Aw hell...* She had tears in her eyes.

"Jade..." He swore under his breath. "I am so sorry, *chica,* I did not mean to treat you poorly. The last thing I want is for you to put me in the same category as your stepfather."

She whipped her head around and wrapped her fingers around his wrist. He looked down at her hand. Such a contrast against his darker skin. He wondered what she would look like draped across him, what his hands would look like on her, the picture her hair would make covering his bare chest. His heart thumped hard, and he ran the back of his finger along her forearm. He couldn't resist. He needed to touch her somewhere. Goose bumps raised in her skin, but she didn't flinch or pull away from the contact. *Hell,* she didn't even finger that damn necklace. Something twisted in his gut when he realized how much he liked that his touch was acceptable to her, but the empty feeling he got when she removed her hand made him clench his teeth. Her touch shouldn't be so important.

"It's not that at all, Han. You make me want...*things.* Things I was perfectly happy doing without before you came along. Things I didn't believe I'd ever want. And I just can't deal with it all. It's too much."

"Then it's probably not the best time to make decisions either. Especially ones that will affect other people. So, this leads me to a crazy idea."

She groaned. "Why am I not surprised? This day will go down in history as the day of crazy ideas. You've sucked me into two of them so far. Are you thinking 'third time's the charm?'"

"Hoping? Praying?" He raised his brows, a teasing smile on his lips as he looked at her. "Are you game?"

If he had to judge by her posture, he'd say, *'No'.* She sat up straight and wrapped her arms around her legs, pulling them to her chest. She squinted her eyes against the glare as she looked at the ocean. Again. Why was she having such a hard time looking at him? More importantly, why the hell did he care?

She barked out a laugh. "You are going to be the death of me, Alejandro Rivera, I swear. What is it with you getting me to be, and do, things I avoid like the plague?"

He stifled a groan. She had the same effect on him. He wasn't sure if that was a good thing or a bad one, but he sure as hell didn't like it. And there was no way he'd let her know it either. Never in his life had he gone to the lengths he had today to be with a woman. Hell, he'd spent less energy getting away from them.

He let out an exasperated breath as a woman walked by them and did a double take, then grabbed his sunglasses from the sand. After putting them on, he pulled the baseball cap from his back pocket and shoved it on his head, yanking the bill down so it shaded his face. Thankfully the woman merely kept walking.

"Spill it."

"Dinner and dancing at The Conga Room."

She said something foul; he tried not to smile.

"You are out of your mind. Not that I wouldn't appreciate the opportunity to have dinner at a place like The Conga Room, but just the thought of being on a dance floor in a crowd gives me the willies."

"Ah, but this is the best part. We can get a VIP room and not have to be *in* the crowd. It's one of my favorite hangouts. I can enjoy dancing, some live music, and not have to worry about being bothered by fans."

She pursed her lips, and he fought the desire to kiss her until she agree to go. He was not going to care whether she accepted his offer or not. This was about Beck's wedding gift, nothing more. He didn't want her to bail on his friend and her sister like she was threatening to.

She bit her lip, and he clenched his hand when he realized he was about to run a soothing finger over the spot her teeth abused. She took a deep breath and he lowered his gaze. His nails bit into his palm as he fought the urge to caress a chest he decided right then was the absolute perfect size.

"So, if we get there, and I decide dancing in public is more than I can handle, you're okay with that?"

Was he? What if this plan backfired too? Time was running out. Could he afford to waste more of it when she wanted out? But how else was he supposed to get her used to the idea of dancing in front of people and help her realize it wasn't something she needed to worry about? He knew she had the talent. Now he needed to find a way to get her past her fears so the talent could shine. *Hell.* He *wanted* to hang out with her at a dance club. And it had nothing whatsoever to do with teaching her to dance for Beck's wedding.

He shrugged to make it look like it didn't matter. "*Sí.*" He cringed inwardly. When Spanish was the first thing out of his mouth, it wasn't a good sign.

"I'll make you a deal. You let me drive your Porsche for the rest of our time together today and I'll go to The Conga Room with you. *If* I can go home and change first. I'm definitely not dressed for a nightclub."

His stomach sank. *No one* drove his Porsche.

"You've got yourself a deal. You're fortunate I

brought it here rather than the truck."

Oh yeah. He was seriously messed up. And he didn't think his stomach could go any lower until they were in his car and she looked at him, gave him a huge grin and chuckled in a way he could only describe as wicked. He groaned, threw his head back against the head rest, and gritted his teeth. "Behave yourself! I've paid for this car with blood, sweat, tears, and more pain than you'll ever experience in your entire life. You wreck it, and I *will* kill you."

She laughed. "Trust me, I know what I'm doing. I'm not going to wreck this beautiful machine. I'm going to savor every minute of driving it. Buckle up." She started the car and looked over at him again. "Han, it's okay. I've had a bit of experience driving sports cars like this. My high school boyfriend taught me a lot about these machines. His father owned a dealership that sold them, and he always had something new and fun to drive from his father's lot."

He looked at her silently for several moments. "That's not helping." He buckled his seat belt. "You might want to get moving before I change my mind."

She gave him another huge smile, put the car in gear and shot away from the curb like a rocket. He *was* going to kill her.

If she didn't kill *them* first.

Though after five minutes as her passenger, he realized he was wrong. She did know what she was doing. *Why had he expected anything less?* To enjoy speeding through traffic like an Indy driver was totally at odds with her uptight personality, yet in another way it wasn't. It was the nature of the accountant to do everything just so, to make sure the numbers add up right. Why would driving be any different? Whatever she took on she would work at until she had it down perfectly. It was her love of driving that surprised him more than how good she was at it. Still, it took him a while to get past the fear of her ruining his precious car—and them with it. All the way to her house in fact.

She looked at him over her shoulder as they entered her apartment and rather than give him his keys, she put them on a hook next to the door. "I am seriously considering stealing your car."

"Is that why you didn't give me my keys?"

"I'm the designated driver for the evening, remember?"

"I better not live to regret it. Now, hurry and get dressed. I'm hungry."

As soon as she left, he prowled around the room, interested in what he could learn about her. To help him with her dance lessons. That was all. Certainly not because he wanted to know her better. That would be stupid. It led nowhere good.

Next to a black leather couch was a full magazine rack, which, judging by that ugly black dress of hers, probably wasn't filled with fashion magazines. Squatting down, he rifled through them. Number puzzle books. All of them. He took one out and flipped through it, then did the same with several more. They weren't easy ones and were all solved. In ink. She really had a thing for numbers. To spend all day working with them and then come home and do number puzzles for entertainment? He was impressed and wondered if she played pool. Being good with numbers could give someone a decided edge in that game. He knew from experience.

He stood and meandered over to a bookshelf. The edge of his mouth quirked up as he swiped a finger along it. As he suspected, no dust. He looked closer at the books. *No way.* Not only were they arranged alphabetically by author, the author's books were arranged alphabetically by title. If he hadn't seen her dance moves in the studio, he'd say she was too left-brain oriented to dance at all. As it was, the puzzles and the organized book shelf were enough to tell him he needed to overcome an instinctive desire to over-analyze her dance moves and think about it all too much. Dancing needed to be felt first.

He turned his attention to the photos on the top shelf in coordinated black frames. There was a picture of a young Jade cuddling an orange tabby cat. The expression on her face told how much she adored the animal. *Damn was she ever adorable.*

He shook his head at himself and quickly looked at the picture next to it. She was a little older, sitting on a couch, with Lexi and a woman who had to be her mother, as she looked a lot like Jade. He didn't like the funny feeling that one gave him, so he moved on. There was one of her and a teenage Lexi at Santa Monica Pier with a couple who looked old enough to be their grandparents. Were they? She'd never mentioned them. Though why would she? But surely she and Lexi would've moved in with them when her mother died if they were. The people who originally owned her business perhaps?

The last one was a picture of her and Lexi with a small group of friends at a restaurant drinking champagne and eating cake. Jade proudly held up what looked to be a diploma. He got another funny feeling in his stomach. He snorted at himself in disgust and threw himself down on the couch. Hanging on the wall to one side of a flat panel television was a print of Picasso's *Hands Holding Flowers*. On the other, a print of William Michael Harnett's *Secretary's Table*. Quite telling.

****

It wasn't until she opened her closet door that she realized finding something suitable to wear might be rather problematic. She had her share of nice clothes, she ran a business after all, but there was a huge difference between business clothes and what she could wear to a place like The Conga Room. Sexy she absolutely did *not* do. Except for her underwear. Which no one could see when she wore it, and thus would never give a man the wrong idea. Theoretically. *Damn you, Alejandro Rivera.*

The fact she had no fashion sense didn't help either. Surely there was something here that would work? Besides the black stilettos, which she pulled out and set on the bed. Probably not very conducive to dancing but then, that wasn't happening, so no worries. She scoured her closet several times over and came up with nothing. Well, almost nothing. A pair of shiny black stretch capris she used for her workout would probably suffice, but as for the top, she'd narrowed down her choices to a plain white blouse or a colorful, semi-casual T-shirt. Deciding the blouse was just too accountant, she went with the T-shirt. It did hug her figure rather flatteringly. She shrugged. It would have to do.

Han stood up from the couch when she joined him in the living room and the expression on his face…Priceless. The way those topaz eyes perused her from head to toe as though he'd touched every inch of her made her skin feel too tight and her heart pound in her ears. After the very thorough once-over, the you-have-got-to-be-kidding-me message came through loud and clear. Did he say it out loud?

"Uh, no. Not happening. Have you no fashion sense? Do you *know* what kind of place The Conga Room is?

"Of course I do, this is my home town, but I don't do the nightlife, bar-scene, party-crowd thing. Therefore, I don't have the requisite—er—sexy wardrobe. Did you seriously think I'd have a leather mini skirt handy?"

He shook his head. Most likely he hadn't thought about it at all. He stood up and looked at her again with his hands on his hips. "You've got the shoes." He eyes darkened. "And the underwear…" His voice petered away, and he swallowed as he looked away for a moment. His face was expressionless when he looked at her again.

Her face, on the other hand, became unbearably hot, though she desperately willed it not to. He knew. He *had* seen down her dress that day. She didn't even know what to say to that. Ignore it seemed the best route. "Yeah, well, Lexi picked out the shoes and…" She looked down at her feet and cleared her throat. "My underwear, *underneath my clothes,* isn't going to give a guy the wrong idea now, is it?"

She looked at him, and he raised his eyebrows but said nothing. He didn't have to. Instead he walked over, placed his hands on her shoulders and turned her around.

"Back to the bedroom. Let's see what I can come up with. In my line of work, I've had quite a bit of wardrobe experience, as well as making do in a pinch."

He flicked back and forth through the clothes in her closet several times before exclaiming, "You have got to be fricking kidding me!"

He turned to her where she sat on the bed watching him, narrowed his eyes and shoved his hands in his pockets. "There's nothing in here but dress slacks, solid color blouses, yoga pants and t-shirts. Never in a million years did I dream I'd spend any length of time with a woman who has a wardrobe like that. Though I didn't see that black dress you were wearing the first time we met."

She crossed her arms and looked at him mutinously.

"Ha! You got rid of it, didn't you?"

She ignored the remark. "Does this mean I don't have to go to The Conga Room?" Her heart sank. Which was stupid, because it really wasn't anything she wanted to do. Seriously.

"Oh, you're going all right. Even if I have to take you shopping first."

"No way. I'm not buying something I will never wear again after tonight. It's the same as flushing money down the toilet."

"Of course not. Practical Jade Nichols would never spend money on something frivolous."

"Are we done here then? You leaving?"

"Not on your life, woman."

His gaze wandered around the room, landing on her dresser, and her stomach knotted. He wouldn't dare go through her underwear and night clothes with her sitting right there. Would he? What would it accomplish?

Before she could stop him, he was at the dresser, pulling open drawers and rifling through them. And laughing. Wickedly. Triumphantly. She wanted to die. He was looking at, *touching,* things no one had seen before. She didn't like the thrill that went through her at the sight of his hands on her underwear, either. Really, she *didn't.* She wasn't going to think about what those hands would look like taking that underwear off of her. She was *not.* Goose bumps broke out all over when she was unable to stop where her mind went. It happened again when he gave another triumphant chuckle. Made her stomach do some crazy acrobatics too before it sank to her toes. He held out a red, lacy camisole, the straps dangling from his forefingers.

"This will do nicely."

"No way. That's a pajama top. I'm not wearing it in public. Besides, my bra will show through it."

"Now you're talking. What color bra are you wearing? If it's red, it's not even going to matter. The lace isn't that see-through. Or you can change into a red one."

"Black." Why the hell had she even answered that question? This was insane.

"Even better. By the way, I love your choices in nighttime attire. It's the day stuff that needs serious work."

She let out a frustrated growl. "You are absolutely out of your mind if you think I'm wearing that camisole with my bra on display anywhere outside of this apartment."

She crossed her arms and gave him a mutinous

look. It didn't help that right then she realized all the crazy sensations zinging around inside her were because he was turning her on. In a bit of a panic, she watched as he flung the top so it landed on the bed next to her and went back to the closet.

"Trust me, you'll be more covered up than most of the women there," he said as he hunted through her closet again. "Here we go." He pulled out a black, iridescent sleeveless blouse, took it off the hanger and threw it at her before returning the empty hanger to the closet. "Wear that over it, but don't button it. With the tight pants and the high heels, you'll do."

Speechless, all she could do was stare at him.

He raised his brows. "Are you going to need my help getting dressed?"

She managed to shake her head. She could've done without that visual. Han, taking off her clothes...

"Take your hair down, too. Just in case I want to run my fingers through it."

And then he was gone, the door closing softly behind him.

****

As soon as he shut the door, he made a beeline for the kitchen. An ice cold glass of water was a desperate attempt to cool himself down. If merely looking at her night clothes and underwear did this to him, what would happen if he saw her dressed in nothing but?

He didn't care if she thought he was rude for looking through her kitchen cupboards and helping himself when she hadn't offered. He was desperate. After finding a glass, he went to the refrigerator to fill it with ice and water from the dispenser on the door, pausing momentarily to shake his head at the calendar

174

and lists neatly lined up on the refrigerator door.

He downed the water, refilled his glass and was ready to take another swallow when she walked in the kitchen. Thank goodness she hadn't come in a millisecond later, or he would have choked on it. She looked so hot he desperately wanted to douse himself with the water instead of drink it. Instead, he slowly lowered the glass and set it on the counter.

"Now we're talking, *chica*." Before he realized it, he'd spoken in his sexy voice. The one he used when he wanted to turn a woman on as much as he was. When he wanted to entice her to do wicked things with him in private.

She took a step back and narrowed her eyes at him. "If the men at this place are going to be looking at me like you are, deal or no deal, I'm not going."

He barely stopped himself from telling her any man that looked at her thinking what he was thinking would end up with a black eye. *He* didn't like knowing he felt that way. *She* certainly wasn't going to know.

"I've already made sure they have a private room for us, so most of the guys there won't be able to see you. No one is going to hassle you. I'll make sure of it. You are not backing out of our deal. You tortured me driving my car; now it's my turn." He grinned and winked, then changed the subject. For his benefit. He was on the verge of doing things he knew he'd regret. For Beck's sake, he couldn't screw this up. "I like your place. The only thing I didn't expect to see here is a Picasso print. His work is so chaotic and you're so...not."

She gave him a cheeky smile. "I know, right? I have no idea why, but I've always liked his stuff."

"Something else we have in common other than the love of my Porsche. Shall we go?"

****

Jade was surprised to realize she was enjoying herself. She felt like a voyeur sitting in their private room with the sliding glass doors closed to keep people out, but the curtains open so they could watch the patrons dancing and enjoying themselves. The flashing lights, the DJ entertaining the crowd, the seventies-esque décor of the place. It was a sight and sound extravaganza, and she'd never experienced anything like it. Even though she was born and raised in L.A. How lame was that?

The food was fantastic. As well as the tequila they currently enjoyed. Though it was a little odd to her that the server wouldn't let them pour their drinks themselves. Still, it hadn't kept them from getting a full glass every time they needed one. She wondered if that might be part of the reason she was enjoying herself so much.

Han wasn't the only celebrity in attendance. She'd glimpsed a few others entering or exiting their own private rooms, and security roamed around looking like the secret service to make sure the glitterati could enjoy themselves hassle-free, as well as keep any altercations from getting out of hand.

She was glad Han forced her into coming. It was a once-in-a-lifetime experience. Though she was tempted to change her mind about that when he tried to convince her to get out on the dance floor.

"*Ai ai ai,* you are the most unusual woman I've ever met. You know how many women here would give anything to dance with Alejandro Rivera?" His tone was incredulous, and it sounded as though he was referring to someone other than himself.

"Everyone but me, most likely." She looked at the glass in her hand and frowned. The trouble was, she wanted to take him up on the offer. A first for her. But she couldn't get past the too-many-people-too-close-together aspect. The thought of being part of the crowd had her hyperventilating. She looked at him and she feared her feelings were written on her face because his countenance softened.

"Ahh, *chica*... You do want to."

Stupid tequila. She slammed her glass down on the table. "I just remembered I'm the designated driver tonight. I need to lay off this stuff and start drinking coffee. As it is, it's going to be a while before I should be driving."

He gave a careless shrug. "I have a limo service in my phone contacts for just such occasions. A little more tequila might loosen you up enough to get you past your issues. Or maybe a lot more. I've been the one doing most of the drinking here."

"Are you suggesting I get drunk?"

Maybe she already had too much. Certainly he wasn't *that* kind of man? She wasn't a bad judge of character. Was she?

"It does have the tendency to lower one's inhibitions."

"That is exactly why I have no desire to do it."

He looked at her and blinked slowly. "You've never been drunk."

"My God, you say it like it's a crime."

He shook his head and looked at her for several moments in silence. "I'm not suggesting you get pass-out drunk. Just slightly…" He waved his drink around and his eyebrows pulled together. "What's the word I want? *Inebriated*. Personally, I think it would do you a world of good."

It was her turn to look at him silently, at a loss for words. Maybe she'd already had too much to drink. "You can't possibly be serious."

He leaned back on the couch and crossed his arms. A smile played about his lips. "Serious as a heart attack, *mi amiga.*"

She snorted in disgust as she too leaned back on the couch that sat perpendicular to the one he was on. "You're insane. What do I have to do to get a server over here? I need to get serious about some coffee so we can go home."

"You're afraid."

"I am not. That's stupid. Why would anyone be afraid of getting drunk? And we're not teenagers, Han. That's the kind of peer-pressure tactics high-schoolers use."

"I'm no high-schooler."

This panther could purr, and the sound of his voice sent a shiver she couldn't suppress from head to toe.

"This is no tactic. I'm stating a fact. You are afraid of getting drunk because you don't want to lose control."

She bit the inside of her cheek to stifle the *damn it* that sprang to her lips. She wasn't necessarily afraid as much as she didn't want to lose control. She *liked* being in control. It made her happy. Truly. "It's about not wanting to have the hangover afterward."

"That's just an added bonus of not over-indulging." He uncrossed his arms and sat up. "Listen, I know how hard it is to feel like your world is out of control, but I also know how freeing it can be to give up control. It's just you and me in our own little world here. I'll make sure you don't do anything stupid."

"Unless, of course, you get drunk, too."

He chuckled. "Then you won't be alone in your stupidity. We'll be stupid together."

"Except that if I get drunk with Alejandro Rivera, it's highly likely the paparazzi—who are crawling all over this place—will share it with the world. Much less anyone who has a camera on their phone."

Her heart thundered in her chest. Was she actually considering something so crazy? It wasn't like he was suggesting she get so wasted she blacked out. Just drunk enough for her to…She put her head in her hands. To be normal. To be able to act like everyone else in the place and go out on the dance floor. That just plain sucked. To need alcohol in order to act like a regular person. But maybe, just maybe, using alcohol to get past her issues this once would make it easier to get past them next time without the liquid courage. For good. But did she want Han to be the one there for her while she tested the waters? Though his idea had merit, it should be Lexi who was the one there for her while she gave it a try.

She bit back a sigh, wiped her hands down her face and sat up straight. Except that right now, for the next several weeks, it was about what Lexi wanted and needed, not about her. Once her sister was married, nothing in Jade's world needed to be about Lexi anymore.

Who was she kidding? Without Han egging her on, she would chicken out. It seemed easier to run from her issues than face them. What was it about Han that made her tired of the running?

She sat up, grabbed her glass and downed its contents in one go, then coughed and thumped her chest.

"Hey, take it easy. Drinking it quickly isn't necessary. This is some nice tequila. Savor it."

She coughed again. "Yeah, I think you're right. Much easier to sip it."

"Sit back, relax and enjoy. I'll make sure you don't overdo it."

"You have no idea what overdoing it for me is. *I* have no idea what that is." She swiped a hand down her face. "What if it doesn't work?"

"No harm done, and you were able to enjoy a mighty fine bottle of tequila."

"I think the mere fact you were able to talk me into this shows I've had too much already."

He laughed softly. "I hope you're not that uptight."

****

He was the one who had too much. Suggesting she drink enough to lose her inhibitions was not one of his better ideas. For her, it worked nicely. For him, well…He would really appreciate some of those inhibitions that made her vigilant about her personal space right about now. He was enjoying the physical contact too much for his own good. And hers. Every fiber of his being screamed for him to indulge himself. To drive her back to his place, give her another shot of tequila and enjoy its after-effects in his bed. Repeatedly. Like he'd done with a hundred other women. Well, not a hundred, and not that he needed to get them drunk to sleep with him, but still…Why in the world was this one different?

Not going there.

And could she dance. A little rough around the edges since she was basically untutored, but if he could get her to dance the same way at the wedding, they'd give them one hell of a show.

Get a grip, Rivera. It's a wedding, not a performance. This wasn't for his television program, for god's sake. He didn't need to put on an award-winning show, and he seriously shouldn't even care. His days for entertaining were over. He'd been doing it since he was a kid, and his life was on a different path now. A path he was completely ready for.

Between the pointers he gave her and the tequila, she was doing the cha-cha-chá like nobody's business. She could shake it with the best of them. Just watching her at arm's length sent rockets off inside him, and when she shimmied up close and personal, it was nearly impossible to continue dancing when all he wanted was to wrap his arms around her, haul her back his house and get down and dirty. So before she could rub against him again, he grabbed her hand and hauled her off the dance floor. Yeah, she hadn't even cared about being on a crowded dance floor.

"It's hot, I need a drink." Talk about lame excuses.

"Aww, but I'm having fun. Don't wanna quit yet."

He blew out a frustrated breath and glanced over his shoulder at her. "It's late and the noise is giving me a headache. This scene is much more fun when you have a few drinks in you and mine wore off long ago."

She tripped along behind him in silence for a few seconds. "'Kay. If you're not feeling good, let's go."

When they reached their room, he slid the doors

and the curtains closed behind them and moved to the back. His sigh of relief died in his throat when he turned around and she was right there. She draped her arms around his neck and leaned into him. His hands automatically landed on her hips, his fingers tightening in an effort to keep them from going anywhere else. How could something so wrong feel so right? She fit perfectly against him, like she was his other half. Thoughts swirled around in his head for a moment, then vanished like they never existed. Blood thundered in his ears, and her voice sounded a long way off.

"Kiss me, Han. A real kiss. Like you never want to stop. I haven't been kissed like that since high school."

With her plastered against him, there was no way he could do anything but. He moved his hands to the small of her back and pressed her into him, half hoping it was enough to scare her off so *she* would put an end to it. They were playing with fire and there was no doubt he'd have burns to show for it.

When she wiggled slightly, the fire burning in his gut snaked through him until every cell was quivering with a need so strong he could hardly breathe. He crushed her lips under his. The rushing, dropping feeling of their first kiss, which he'd blamed on the movement of the elevator, engulfed him. *Hell*...It was *her*. The feel, the taste, the scent. Not the elevator at all.

He made a guttural noise and wrapped his arms around her, pulling her closer in a futile attempt to make her part of him. He needed her to be his. *Now.* But it was more than that. He ached with the need to be part of her, one with her. If it'd been humanly possible, he would've gladly climbed inside her. It seemed the only way to fill the aching need inside him. It was foreign, even a bit frightening, but worse than that, he sensed the only way he could truly be whole, to find real peace, was to lose himself in her.

As torturous as it was to drag himself out of that place, all he could do was thank God for the server's voice asking if they needed anything from the other side of the door.

He disentangled himself from her, desperately hoping she didn't see how his hands were shaking. He stepped back a pace and clasped them behind his back. His voice came out as a croak.

"Could you bring us the check?"

Damn was she gorgeous. Her cheeks were flushed; her eyes sparkled with desire. He ground his teeth together and clenched his hands more tightly to stop himself from pulling her back in his arms, from exploring every inch of her with his hands and mouth. His gaze was snared by the heaving of her chest as she breathed like she'd run a marathon, and tantalizing glimpses of white skin through black and red lace grabbed his attention. He closed his eyes to block out the sight in a desperate attempt to keep his hands to himself.

His voice was husky with his desire no matter what he did to prevent it. "I've never taken advantage of a woman who's had too much to drink and I'm not about to start now. Time to call it quits, *chica.*"

Chapter Eleven

"No way. No. Fricking. Way."

Hands on hips, Jade wore a mutinous look on her face. Han clenched his jaw to stop words clamoring to get out, however he couldn't help the glare. Damn, was she good at pushing his buttons. He *knew* she'd react like this, prepared himself even, and he was still thoroughly annoyed. He'd waited until the end of their lesson to spring it on her, hoping the vast improvements she'd made would help her appreciate her new skills.

"I've been taking lessons for a month and you think I can *perform* on stage?" She marched over to the bench and with jerky movements started removing her shoes; the ones she planned to wear for the wedding. "You know, Han, sometimes I really hate you."

"I know." He chuckled and his ire disappeared. "Your complete lack of regard for my celebrity status is one of the things I love about you, *chica*. The only people who dare tell me to shove it since Marguerite died are you and Cat."

His voice petered away, and he sucked in a breath like the words burned his tongue. Had he really just uttered the *L* word? He barely suppressed his own, *No fricking way.* Turning his back on her, he crossed his arms, prowled across the room and threw his head back to stare at the ceiling. He didn't do *love*. That wasn't what he meant. Never in a million years. He decided when Marguerite died, it wasn't worth the pain. He lowered his head and silently cursed Beck for bringing this woman into his life. And he just told her he wanted to do a dance performance with her at his fundraiser? He swore violently in Spanish under his breath.

"No reason to get so worked up, Han. I'm sure you have plenty of girls to choose from."

He didn't turn around; he couldn't. He didn't dare look at her, and it took all his control to keep his voice neutral. "Not plenty, but the person who was going to do it with me has canceled for a family emergency." He took a deep breath, berating himself for being such an idiot, and crossed his arms as though it would protect him from feeling anything. He turned to face her. "You, whether you believe it or not, are extremely talented, and I would like to highlight at the fundraiser another aspect of how dancing can help someone. It's helped you with your emotional issues. And don't tell me it hasn't."

She lifted her chin. "Oh. My. God. Not only do you want to put my dancing on display, but how screwed up I am as well? You need your head examined." She paused and chewed her lower lip for a moment. "I'm sure I'm not your only possibility. Pick someone else. How about Cat?"

"My dance studios are not just for kids. And you misunderstand. I'm not going to reveal anything personal about you. I want adults to see they can benefit from learning to dance as well."

He dropped his arms, crossed the room and sat next to her. He needed to get over himself, ignore his feelings. Acting on feelings only caused trouble. This was for Let's Dance and the kids who benefited from having such a place to escape reality. It wasn't about him.

"You are the one for the job, Jade. We'll do a cha-cha, to one of your favorite songs if you like. I know you can cha-cha like nobody's business; I've seen it first-hand. It won't take much to get you ready and teach you the routine. I'll keep it fairly simple, since you won't have a lot of time to work on it."

She rubbed her hands down her face, then propped her chin on them and looked at him, the mental battle plainly written on her face. He scooted closer to her, but not so close their legs touched, and caressed her back with his hand, ignoring the fire that raced up his arm at the contact. If only he could fan it until it consumed them...*Stop it.*

"*Chica.*" He ran his fingers lightly down her arm and took her hand in his. "You are so close to moving on with your life unhindered. You need this. I need this. We will be helping each other, all for a worthy cause."
She looked at him, and he suppressed a wince. If eyes could bite, consider himself bitten.

"How could I not get over any issues I have after being around you? I swear, you have touching OCD or something. Do you ever keep your hands to yourself?"

He shrugged a shoulder, tightened his grip on her hand and grinned unrepentantly. "I'm a tactile person." He moved his leg so that their thighs barely touched. "It's a good thing, and you can't fool me. I know you like it."

Her only answer was a glare.

"I have an idea. Do you have some time right now?"

"I'm not sure I want to answer that."

186

He blew out an exasperated breath, then tucked a wisp of her hair behind her ear. "You need to see what I see when you dance. I think it will boost your confidence."

She looked at him askance. "You're just flattering me to get me to do what you want."

"I don't flatter my dance students. I flatter the women I want to sleep with."

She rolled her eyes. "All right. I'll let you give it a shot. I'm curious about the lengths you'll go to get what you want. With someone who isn't bowled over by who you are."

"Damn, you're hard on a man's ego." He made an exasperated noise and ran a finger down her cheek. "Come with me to my office." He stood and pulled her to her feet with the hand he still held.

****

When she entered the office close on his heels and saw the window that looked out onto the dance studio, she made a choking noise and prayed he didn't hear it. Had he watched her dancing that first day? Had the Devil of the Dance Floor seen her shake her bootie? Could there be anything more humiliating? Not even dancing at the fundraiser seemed worse. She put her hands to her hot cheeks and quickly looked around the room before he figured out what she was thinking.

After taking in a desk and a flat panel television hanging on one wall, her eyes landed on a display case with several trophies. She walked over and looked at them, mostly because it gave her a reason to keep her back towards him and regain her composure. What she really wanted to do was crawl under his big black desk and hide.

She perused the trophies and tried to calm her heartbeat by reading their inscriptions. About ten years ago Han had been a ballroom and Latin dance champion in several different, renowned competitions all over the world. Which reminded her exactly who this guy was and brought her right back to feeling embarrassed. And it didn't settle her heart rate.

"Rather impressive collection you have here."

He lifted one shoulder. "I have lived and breathed dancing most of my life and it's paid me back generously. So when I say you've got talent, I know what I'm talking about." He made a sweeping gesture to the television where a recording of her dancing before their first lesson started to play. "Look, you can see what I mean."

Her cheeks burned. He'd not only watched her, but recorded her too? "Oh my God, Han...No. Just...No." She felt his gaze on her but refused to look at him.

"Do not feel embarrassed, Jade. I record everyone, even myself. It helps me see where work needs to be done. It's nothing but a tool of the trade."

Her eyes flicked to him in disbelief before returning to the video, and after several moments of watching in silence, she had to concede he was right. When she pretended she wasn't watching herself, she could see that she had natural grace and wasn't just awkwardly moving to the music.

"It's hard to believe that's what I look like on the outside. It's not at all how I feel on the inside when I'm doing it."

She swallowed a lump that suddenly appeared in her throat. Was he really asking so much of her? If this was what she looked like, then she wasn't going to be making a fool of herself, which was what she feared most. She threw herself down on one of the chairs and crossed her arms. Han turned off the video and sat behind his desk, the leather of his chair creaking as he leaned back in it and crossed his arms.

Even if the time he spent with her was because of a gift to his best friend, it didn't minimize all he'd done for her and Lexi. And he had no idea what he was taking on when he offered the gift to Beck. He'd been more than generous with his time and efforts so far so she could dance at her sister's wedding. How could she not do this thing he was asking of her? She really owed him a lot more than that.

"I'll do it."

"Really? I expected more of a fight."

She shrugged a shoulder. "You're the expert. If you're confident I won't ruin the reputation of your dance studio, I'll bow to your better judgment. And like you say, it's a worthy cause. When do we start?"

He uncrossed his arms, blew out a breath and sat up in his chair. "The fundraiser is the Saturday before the wedding. How much time do you have to work on this? You still need to get the routine down for the wedding party dance and then we need to practice it with Beck and Lexi." He drummed his fingers on the desk. "Now that I think about it, maybe I'm asking too much. You have your own business to run and there may not be enough time."

She raised her brows. "Having second thoughts now? You've gone to all this trouble to talk me into this, and now *you're* backing out?"

He glanced at her briefly before he turned his attention back to his fingers and drummed them faster for a moment. Then he steepled his hands and tapped his forefingers together. "As soon as I knew I needed someone to do this, you came to mind. I just didn't think through the logistics of it."

"Fortunately for you, quarterlies aren't due right now. And since I knew I'd be busy for the wedding, I made sure my schedule was pretty light until afterward. I'm only working three days a week for the next month. Besides, I'm not a one-man show. I have two other employees."

"Ah, *bueno!*"

He smiled brilliantly and if he'd done that when he first asked her to do this, she would've agreed immediately. She frowned. That couldn't be good.

He relaxed back into his chair. "When can you start?"

"Tomorrow work for you?"

****

Han sat in his hot tub, easing away the aches and pains from a day of hard physical work, sipping a glass of Merlot and trying to figure out what in the world had gotten into him. He frowned darkly at his glass before taking a long swallow, then refilled it from the bottle perched near the edge of the tub.

His gut told him he should stay away from Jade, yet here he was signing on for more time with her. Not that she wasn't the exact person he wanted for the dance routine; he hadn't made that up. And he reluctantly acknowledged it wasn't the perfectionist in him that asked her to do it. He wanted her to be his dance partner on stage more than he ever wanted anyone or anything. Which should've been reason enough for him to run like a mad man in the opposite direction. There were plenty of other people who could get the job done. He frowned again and took another big swallow of the fine wine, doing it an injustice in the process.

Had a woman ever dominated his thoughts the way she did? No, unless it was related to dance. And if the woman had nothing to do with dancing, then thoughts of her never interfered with his work. Why was it so different with Jade?

He snorted in disgust, set his glass next to the wine bottle and slipped under the water for a moment in an effort to wash her out of his head. Sitting back up, he brushed his hair back out of his eyes and ran his hands down his face to wipe away the water. He finished off the wine in his glass and decided to stop there. He'd polish off the bottle when he wasn't under the influence of the hot tub.

He laid his head back and closed his eyes. What he needed was to take her to bed for a week straight. Get her out of his system so he could focus again. That was really the root of the problem. It was the first time he'd ached so much for a woman and not acted on it. And it was exactly why he made sure he never went within a mile of a woman he suspected required more than something physical. It complicated things and he *loathed* complications. He'd had more than his fair share and had made an art of avoiding all things complicated.

Which settled the unease of his obsession with Jade but led him to dwelling on what getting physical with her off the dance floor would be like. No less disturbing than the emotional mess she'd brought on him, but easier to deal with. As soon as the wedding was over, he was going to pursue her in a whole different way. To hell with the fact she wasn't his usual type. He needed her out of his system once and for all, and it was the only way he knew to do it.

****

"No, no, *no!*" The Devil of the Dance Floor barked at her for the millionth time. And this was definitely *The Devil of the Dance Floor*. Han had vanished five minutes after they entered the dance studio.

"That's not going to make me get it right. No matter how many times you say it."

He prowled across the room, picked up a towel and ran it over his face and down his bare chest, before slinging it around his neck. It had her thinking of an exotic black panther again, all glowing yellow eyes and rippling muscles. But actually, his glorious, half-dressed physique wasn't what her problem was. Well, mostly. The problem was she couldn't turn off her head. She knew the routine by heart but kept second-guessing every step she made. It was no secret it was driving Han crazy, but it made her nuts, too.

"You have *got* to turn off your head and feel the dance."

"Really, Han? That's the secret? Because I didn't realize that from the hundred other times you've told me today. Or yesterday, or the day before that. Looks like you've found a hole in your teaching skills." He muttered something in Spanish and she wished he said it a little louder so she knew what it was. Then she looked at his face and decided not to ask him to speak up. She was better off not knowing. Still, she couldn't stop the words that came out of her mouth, though it had to be the worst time ever to say them. "Be careful,

192

Han; I speak fluent Spanish."

His startled gaze went to her face; then his expression froze. "Would've been nice to know that sooner." He ripped the towel off his neck, turned his back towards her, and pitched it at the laundry bin. She braced herself for what came next. "What you need is some tequila to turn off that analytical brain of yours. I realize dancing uses a lot of counting, but you're obsessing over it."

She relaxed. If he was going to ignore her revelation, then she would too. They had more important things to take care of, but Han's suggestion was not the answer. "I need tequila to cope with my *teacher*. And I never thought I'd say this, but I am *so* close to being thoroughly sick of that song. And it was one of my favorites."

He walked back across the room with a towel for her, stopping just short of entering her personal space. Though at this point, there was no such thing as personal space around him. He gave her the towel, and she wiped herself down with it.

"What other music makes you want to move?" he asked in Spanish.

Her mouth opened involuntarily, and she closed it quickly when she realized it. So he didn't believe she knew Spanish. Her gaze darted to his face, wondering what kind of idea had popped in his head. She told him in Spanish some of her favorite artists. "I don't see how changing the music will turn off my brain."

Was that admiration that flashed in his eyes? He cleared his throat and smoothed a strand of hair off her face. "That's one sexy accent you've got…"

If it wasn't for the shiver that streaked down her

spine at the contact, she wouldn't have thought twice about it. Hopefully, after all this, anyone could touch her, and she wouldn't have a meltdown. If that turned out to be the case, then everything Han was putting her through would be worth it.

He reverted to English. "I want to give it a try. I know a couple of songs that work with the routine." He walked over to the sound system and got the music ready. "Here's hoping." He stepped up to her and held out his hand. She took it. "Ready?"

"To throw in the towel? Yes. To dance? Do I have a choice?"

"No." He narrowed his eyes for a moment. "I want you to feel the music and the beat. Concentrate on the words if it helps."

"Yes. I know. You said that already. Repeatedly."

This time he rolled his eyes, and she realized she wasn't the only one stressed out about how hard it was for her. So when the music started, she made the attempt again. And it actually worked. Somewhat. The change of song helped because she wasn't so accustomed to the music she no longer heard it. Unfortunately, it was in spurts. Her head would turn off for a few measures and then before she realized it, she was counting the beats, thinking about the next step, where her hands should be, what she looked like when she was shaking her bootie.

"Progress," he conceded when the song ended, but didn't look pleased with it. He put his hands on her shoulders, then absently ran them up and down her arms. "Let's try something else. You like those modern remakes of vintage music the best?"

She looked at him, conflicted. She wanted to do the

dance right, was willing to do what she had to do to make it perfect. But she was loathe to admit how much she enjoyed that kind of music. It was so…Corny. And very *un*-hip.

"*Sí?* Lexi says this is so."

She blew out a breath in exasperation. "Yes. I know, it's lame."

"*Como?* I think it fits you. There's some great dance music and I enjoy it too. Any particular ones you like better than the others?"

She shrugged. "Not really."

"I'll queue up a few. We are going to simply dance. Like at the club. No routine, no particular dance style. Just moving to the music. You following my lead. *Sí?*"

"I'll try anything at this point. I probably want this perfect more than you do."

"Hard to say. We're both still here at eight o'clock at night, no dinner and no intention of leaving any time soon."

The music started, he pulled her close and that was when she knew she was in big trouble. She didn't think about her feet and where they should go next; she didn't think about her frame; she didn't think about the count. She could only feel, and her mind was stuck on the sensations. How his touch felt so incredibly right. Like it had when they danced at The Conga Room. So it wasn't the tequila. It was him. And she knew she should be worried about that, but she wasn't. Not when she was feeling so…*Much.*

The music throbbed around them, around her. Through them, through her, and became a living thing that took her control. Control she surrendered willingly.

Because not having it felt so…*right*.

She wasn't exactly sure when the dancing turned into outright foreplay. It was before she realized how turned on Han was. Before he started running his hands along her back. And long before he bent his head, captured her mouth and devoured it like he'd been celibate for years. She had no idea when they stopped moving to the music or when he backed her against the wall. Her brain was off with no intention of coming back on any time soon. And it didn't frighten her—it freed her. The bubble was gone, obliterated by the avalanche of sensations aroused by Han's…*everything*. Because of him she'd done a one-eighty; from cringing at a touch to dreading its absence. And tequila had nothing to do with it this time.

He pressed her into the wall, still moving rhythmically to the music and as his hands cradled her head, she wished her hair was loose so he could thread his fingers through it. He unleashed a maelstrom inside her, making her desperate for more, never wanting him to *stop* touching her. His hands left her head to caress her neck, then down her arms and back up. How could she have ever dreaded something so heavenly?

Her brain came back on with a vengeance and she froze for a moment before struggling frantically to be free; kicking and hitting in an effort to regain her personal space, to make it all *go away*. Han let her go like she burned and moved away to lean against the wall next to her, his breathing audible, hands clenched at his sides.

"Damn, *chica*."

His voice was thick and rough and even in her panic, made her melt inside. Brought her back to where she was and who she was with.

"I am *so* sorry. I swear, I never meant things to go so far. I would never, *ever* force you to do anything. But you are one hot mama made for loving." He cleared his throat. "Are you okay?"

She nodded and squeezed her eyes shut. *He* wasn't the one who should be sorry, and she couldn't bring herself to open her eyes and look at him. Instinctively her fingers went to her neck, wanting to grab her locket. It wasn't there. She'd given up wearing it during her lessons long ago and hadn't needed it until now. She'd been happy about that. Until now.

She had to swallow before she could speak. "There's absolutely no need for you to apologize, Han. I'm the one in the wrong. For teasing you. It's my fault we can't finish what we started." She opened her eyes, ran a shaky hand over the top of her head and down along her braid, bit the inside of her lip. "I—thanks for respecting my wishes." She covered her face with her hands. "You have no idea how much I wish things were different."

"Oh, I'm pretty sure I do. I don't think I've wanted anything more than I want you right now."

She dropped her hands to her side, pressed them into the wall and turned her head to look at him. His fisted hands pressed into his thighs. Her gaze traveled upwards to a well-muscled abdomen that moved rapidly with his deep breaths, then moved quickly on, over his chest and came to a stop at his face. Looking at his physique had her wanting things she knew she wouldn't be able to follow through on. His jaw was clenched, a sheen of sweat covered his brow and upper lip, and his eyes were twin flames that threatened to devour her, to drag her back where she didn't dare go. She was not a tease, and she wasn't going to experiment with him to see how far they could go before she panicked again.

"I think it's time we called it quits. I'll be back the day after tomorrow, which should give us time to cool down enough to practice *dancing*."

"Oh no you don't. We've made some significant progress, and there's no way I'm letting you leave and give you time to revert back. I just need a minute to cool down. And now that I know you're not freaked out by how much you turn me on, we can dance without my having to be careful you don't notice it."

"Oh my God…So the trouble we've been having getting this right isn't just my fault after all."

He pushed himself away from the wall and barked out a laugh as he walked across the room and grabbed his water bottle. After taking a long swallow he said, "Though my tension in that regard may have communicated itself to you, it still all goes back to your issues, Sweetheart. You are not pinning any of this on me." He set the water bottle down, started the music and held a hand out to her. "No more worrying about— er—inappropriate contact. We are not leaving tonight until you get it right."

Chapter Twelve

A tight grip on the strap of her purse, Jade knocked on Lexi's door. She didn't usually drop in out of the blue, not since her sister began seeing Beck, but she hadn't told her about the fundraiser and if she left it any longer, Lexi would be pissed.

Why hadn't she told her right away? She normally didn't keep secrets from her. As she waited for her to answer the door, Jade wished she hadn't given in to the impulse to drop by on her way home. She should've just called.

"Jade! What are you doing here?" Lexi shook her head at herself. "Not that I'm not happy to see you. Come in." She moved back and opened the door all the way.

Jade stepped inside and made her way to the living room, picking her way through a variety of shoes, as Lexi closed the door and followed her.

"Geez, Lex, how can you live in such a mess? You know it's little things like bad housekeeping that can drive a man away. Does Beck know you don't like cleaning?"

Lexi rolled her eyes. "Talk about archaic thinking, and you can stop being my mother, Jade. I've been an adult for quite some time now, and I don't need you acting like one anymore." She blew out a breath. "Of course, Beck knows. I don't keep secrets from him.

Besides, he's rich, remember? He has a housekeeper whom we're keeping on after we're married."

The reality of the situation hit her, and Jade's heart ached for a moment. Lexi didn't need her anymore, and Jade could no longer ignore it. It wasn't just the two of them now. She had Beck, and *he* was the center of her universe. She swallowed the lump in her throat, and her eyes burned. Soon she'd be all alone.

"Right, sorry. Old habits."

Lexi shook her head at herself. "I didn't mean to snap at you; I'm just starting to feel a bit swamped by everything I have to do in the next few weeks. The thought of packing up my entire apartment is overwhelming."

"I can imagine. And I'd say I'm here to do whatever you need me to, however…" Her voice petered away, and she cleared her throat, unsure how to tell her about the fundraiser.

"What? What's going on? Are you okay?"

She walked over to the couch, pushed aside a magazine and sat down. "Han asked me to do a dance routine with him at a fundraiser in a couple weeks."

"What? And you're just now telling me? God, are you ever going to stop treating me like a child? I'm your *sister,* Jade. You can tell me stuff like this. I had no idea you could dance well enough Han would want you to perform with him."

"You've got enough going on right now, and I didn't want to bother you with my junk."

"And that is exactly what I mean by your treating me like a child. Sisters bother each other with their *junk*. They have each other's backs. It's not a one way street. You deserve someone to talk to, too. Did it ever occur to you that I want to be there for you in the same way you are for me? But you never let me, and you've got it so together, most of the time I feel like I have nothing to offer anyway."

"Lexi, I never knew…"

"Probably because you're so busy taking care of me, you never thought I'd like to take care of you, too. Don't get me wrong, you've done an amazing job stepping in after Mom was gone. I don't think I can ever repay you, but did you ever think about the fact I lost a sister when it happened? I miss having a big sister, Jade." She dropped down on the couch next to her and took her hand. "God, I'm so glad I got that off my chest. I've been wanting to say it for so long."

Jade squeezed her hand. "I'm sorry. I can't believe I never thought of it like that. Now that you've brought it to my attention, though, I rather miss having a sister, too. Although I'm not sure I know how to be one after all this time."

"Easy peasy. First of all, tell me all about this performance you're doing and how that happened. When is it? There's no way I'm missing it, no matter what I have to cancel. My God, Jade, you're dancing with Alejandro Rivera on stage! Is he as sexy to dance with as it looks on TV?"

Jade laughed. She may not be ready to talk with her sister about *how* sexy Han was, but she was definitely going to like this sister thing.

****

Her mind was completely blank and her heart pounded so hard she was sure everyone around her heard it. She thought the costume—a red dress with a floaty, shimmery skirt and a tight sequin-covered bodice—made her look horribly skinny. Everyone else, including Han, said it made her look *sexy*. No matter who was right, it wasn't a look she wanted to put on display for a theater full of people. Mostly it compounded the dread she felt at going on stage in a real theater where thousands of eyes would be watching her. The fact her mind had gone blank helped in that regard, but it posed a problem for doing the dance routine.

Han's hands descended on her shoulders and turned her to face him as they waited in the wings for their cue. He moved his hands to either side of her neck and tilted her head up with his thumbs under her chin.

"Jade, you're going to do fine. Just keep your eyes on mine. I will guide you, and if you mess up, I can fix it. Stop worrying about them." He tilted his head towards the audience. "Remember what this is for. You're helping Cat. As well as the many other kids who could use a break. Who just need someone to give them a chance. Focus on *that*."

She nodded her head slightly, then his lips were on hers and gone before she had a chance to respond. Absently she wiped the red lipstick off his lips with her thumb. "How can you be so calm? Aren't you nervous *at all*?"

He shook his head, and his eyes sparkled, rivaling the sequins on his red shirt for brightness. A shirt that was only buttoned halfway up his chest. She had to force herself to not look at or think about that.

"I grew up on this, *chica*. It feels like home to me. Makes me feel alive. I am excited for the world to see what I see when you dance. You are going to bring down the house."

"Now you're just flattering me so I'll do a good job of it. I'm too much of a novice to get that kind of reaction."

"I already told you, I only flatter girls I want to sleep with."

She raised her brows at him. "If I remember correctly, I'm one of those girls…"

He rolled his eyes. *"Ai ai ai!* You are such a piece of work." He tilted his head back, looked at the ceiling for a moment then returned his attention to her. "That's our cue. Let's go."

He'd done such a good job distracting her that when they went out on stage and started their number, habit took over and she automatically danced the routine. The music coursed through her as she moved. Han's confidence rubbed off on her, and she forgot where they were. It was the thunderous applause as they left the stage that reminded her.

"Was I right, or was I right?"

Before she could say anything, he took her in his arms and kissed her so thoroughly the noise of the audience, as well as the chaos of backstage, faded away. It took her a moment to regain her equilibrium when he raised his head and focused his bubbly, champagne-gaze on her.

"I'm pretty sure that's the standard audience response after watching Alejandro Rivera dance."

"That is for *us,* Jade. Whether you wish to believe it or not." He put his hands on her hips and pulled her close, pressing his hips into hers, holding her there for several long beats. The fire smoldering deep within her, kept at bay and ignored while she was shimmying against him on stage, roared to life and left her quivering.

Made her ache for things she knew she could never have. She closed her eyes for a moment, savoring the sensations, the closeness, the power she had over a man like him. The strength he'd shown by not acting on the way she made him feel. She took a deep shaky breath in an effort to stifle a desire she couldn't do anything about and opened her eyes.

"Watching you out there did this to me, and no doubt to plenty of other men in the audience as they watched your sexy dance moves. And I'm sorry if it freaks you out, but it's a good thing. *You* made the audience feel good, just as much as I did. And you know what happens when people feel good?"

She mutely shook her head. She was pretty sure she couldn't speak to save her life.

He let her go, took a step back and treated her to a killer, Alejandro Rivera smile. "They spend money. And they will be spending it on Let's Dance." His expression sobered, became serious. "How can I ever pay you back for that, Jade?" He grabbed her hand and started pulling her behind him, away from the stage, to make room for the people waiting for their cue to go on next and headed to the dressing rooms.

"You don't owe me anything," she told him when they paused outside the women's dressing room. "You took on a lot more than you bargained for when you offered Beck and Lexi dance lessons as a wedding present."

She looked down at her feet and swallowed the lump in her throat. One more week and her time with Han would be over. She thought two months was going to be an eternity, but instead, it flew by. She blinked away sudden tears at the thought she'd rarely, if ever, see him after next weekend. "I'm the one indebted to you. You were the final piece to setting me free, Han. I can never pay you back for that."

He ran a finger down her cheek, his eyes dark and unreadable. "I don't want to be paid back, *mi amiga*. It's not about that. It was never about that." He gave her a half smile. "You better change your clothes while it's not so crowded in there." He nodded his head, gave her a wink before he turned away and walked down the hall, disappearing behind the door of his private dressing room.

Jade shook her head to rid herself of the vision of him stripping off his clothes behind that door and entered the dressing room.

A week from now, Lexi would be married, no longer in need of her, Beck's responsibility instead, and suddenly her life looked very lonely. She sighed as she undid the zipper on her dress. It wasn't Lexi she'd be missing. What kind of cruel joke was it that the one man whose touch made her feel alive was the one man she could never have?

Grateful for the emptiness of the dressing room and the opportunity to be alone, she slowly started removing her costume. She wasn't going to cry. She'd cried plenty since her mother died, and she didn't indulge in it anymore. She should be thankful. Her sister was marrying a wonderful man. Lexi was a happy, well-grounded adult, and Jade was now free to go anywhere and do anything she wanted without the financial or emotional responsibility of her younger sister. And thanks to Han, she now knew she could handle a romantic relationship of her own. She no longer cringed at the thought of a man getting close to her. She wasn't tied to her locket like she used to be. She was sure, if she loved the guy, the last of her barriers would crumble.

She sniffed at the tickle in her nose. Things were looking up. She had absolutely no reason to be sad. She was just crashing from the adrenaline rush of performing.

She jumped at the knock on the dressing room door. Since she'd changed out of her costume and was ready to leave, she grabbed her purse as she went to answer it. Whoever it was wasn't looking for her, and all she wanted was to go home and savor the solitude. It was a shock to see Han standing there.

"I hope you weren't planning on leaving? You *are* going to stay for the rest of the show, right?"

She bit her lip. "Actually…" She swallowed. As much as she wanted to go home, she didn't want to miss Cat's performance.

"I'd like you to stay, but if you need to leave…" He shrugged a shoulder as though it didn't matter to him one way or the other, which solidified her desire to go home. "I'm sure as the maid of honor the week before the wedding you've got a lot to do. We do have to figure out our practice schedule for this week, though. Walk with me while we talk about it? I need to hunt through the costume closet for a head-piece. One of the little girls who's performing misplaced the original. Typical kind of show-time catastrophe." He smiled.

"Sure. But don't they have people here to take care of things like that? You're the star of the show."

He chuckled. "Comes with the territory sometimes,

especially in a performance like this one with a significantly smaller budget. Everyone pitches in, and since my act is done, I'm free to be the errand boy. Come on, we need to be quick."

She stepped out of the room, closed the door behind her, and they headed down the hall. It was one of the few times she was grateful for long legs that made it easy for her to keep up with him.

"So we have the final rehearsal on Thursday night for our dance, as well as Lexi and Beck's. They've worked hard, and I'm happy with the results. How comfortable are you with our routine? Lexi wants one more lesson for both dances before the final run-through, and I was wondering about you." He stopped at the door to a closet and unlocked it, then swung it open and looked at her over his shoulder. "What do you think you'll need?"

"After today's performance, the wedding seems like a piece of cake, but I would like to do one more practice session. How about Wednesday? We have the bachelor and bachelorette parties that evening, but I'm only working on Monday, so I can come in sometime earlier in the day, before I do the last minute party stuff."

Han nodded his head and flicked on the closet light. It was rather spacious for a closet but was jam-packed with props and every kind of accessory imaginable. And totally unorganized. Which baffled Jade as well as bugged her. Wouldn't it be so much easier to have it organized so people could quickly find what they needed when they needed it?

"Damn, what a mess! Come in here and help me, would you?"

"Sure. What are we looking for?" She stepped in the closet with him, closing the door partially behind her.

"Don't you dare close that door."

"Chill out, Han. I'm just getting it out of the way. It opens into the hall and people run down it like maniacs. I don't want anyone to get hurt."

"Right, sorry. Momentary panic."

"What are we looking for?"

"Something pink and flowery for a little girl to wear on her head. It can be a clip, a headband, a crown. As long as it's pink and not too big for a child to wear."

Han started rummaging through things, haphazardly moving stuff out of the way, and she appreciated how the closet came to be in such disarray. There was no time to keep things neat when you needed something immediately.

Both of them picked up several items and discarded them as too big, and they were back in the depths of the closet when Jade finally came across something she thought would work. As she did so, the heavy metal door closed with a resounding *thunk*. Han smothered a curse but quickly pulled himself together.

"Someone must be in a hurry," Jade said in an effort to ease the tension and held up a barrette with a sparkly pink rose on it. "What do you think of this?"

"Perfect." He took it and strode over to the door. "We have about two minutes to get it to her and put it on." He turned to face her. "So Wednesday morning work for you?"

She nodded. "That's fine. With the party that day, I haven't scheduled anything other than my usual workout."

He rested his hand on the door knob and looked over his shoulder at her. "Ten o'clock?"

"That should be fine."

She jumped when he rattled off a string of Spanish expletives and banged a fist on the door. "Please tell me we're not locked in here."

He hammered on the door again then turned around, leaned against it and covered his eyes with a hand for a moment.

"Door locks from the outside and whoever shut it didn't bother to make sure no one was inside first." He made a frustrated noise. "You have your cell phone in your purse? Mine is in my dressing room."

"I do." She opened her bag and started rummaging around for it. "I hope you know what number to call."

"*De nada.* I can call the main office and they should be able to get a hold of someone. Though somebody may come looking for me here since they're waiting on me for what they need. Let's give it a few minutes before I make the call. Otherwise, they'll be doing the number without the hair decoration." He set it on a nearby shelf, trying to appear careless, but she saw him clench and unclench his hand.

"Hope the little girl doesn't take it too hard if that's the case." She grabbed her cell phone and pulled it out, ready if he decided to use it.

"Yeah. That was the main reason I offered to find her something. She was pretty worked up about losing the one she was supposed to wear. It's not that big of a deal. This sort of thing is par for the course."

He leaned back against the door and crossed his arms. Suddenly he chuckled. Considering they were locked in a closet and he was claustrophobic, it caught her by surprise. Her eyes flew to his face. He wasn't fooling her. The tightness around his eyes and mouth gave him away. Still, she admired his control.

"I hope our getting stuck in small places isn't going to become a habit."

Jade laughed. It was rather funny that in the space of a couple months she found herself trapped with Alejandro Rivera twice. "What are the odds? Are you going to flip out on me again?"

He groaned. "Used to be, I'd have no problem, but after that elevator episode…" He shrugged like it wasn't a big deal, but Jade suspected otherwise. "I've regressed so this is good for me, actually. I can practice my coping skills." He cleared his throat and uncrossed his arms. "I need a distraction, I think. Focusing on where I'm at makes it worse." He pushed himself away from the door and took a step towards her. "You care to help me think about other things? You did a pretty good job of it last time."

She narrowed her eyes at him. "I'm not sure what you mean by that."

"Exactly what you're afraid I mean."

His hands landed on her hips, and he pulled her up against him. "This time there's no personal space bubble to worry about, so you can distract me the way I wanted you to in the elevator."

He wrapped his arms around her, put a hand in the small of her back, and threaded the fingers of his other one through her hair. Then he kissed her like he needed it to survive, creating an ache in her so deep and strong she moaned from the intensity of it, her heart pounding so hard and fast it left her light-headed.

How was it possible for one man to have so much

power over her? It was thrilling, it was mind-blowing, it was everything she needed and wanted in a kiss. And it scared the crap out of her. There was no future in this. She wasn't going to be one of a long list of Alejandro Rivera's ex-lovers. As glorious, as *right* as it felt to be held like this, be kissed like this, the only outcome of giving in to the momentary pleasure was pain when he moved on. And she didn't need any more pain, certainly not when she had the power to avoid it.

She wriggled, trying to move out of his arms, but it didn't get the reaction she hoped for. Han removed his lips with a groan, his accent thick and so sexy she momentarily forgot her intentions.

"*Ai ai ai* , do that some more, *chica*." He mimicked her movements and started kissing her neck. Her head spun, and she forced herself back to reality. She may be ready for a relationship, but she wasn't ready for a fling. In fact, she was pretty sure a fling was something she'd never be ready for. And definitely not in the storage closet of a theater.

"Han, you have to stop. I'm not the kind of girl to have a quickie in a closet. I'll never be that kind of girl. Your kind of girl."

He stiffened like she'd dumped a bucket of cold water on him before he dropped his arms and stepped away from her. His hands fisted at his sides, and his jaw clenched and unclenched as he looked at her in silence.

He drew in a long breath through his nose. "You are right. I am a love-them-and-leave-them kind of guy, and the women I hook up with not only know it but want the same. It's the only sort of relationship I want. Ever." He unclenched his hands and raked his fingers through his hair, then turned and banged a fist on the door several times.

"Hey! Someone open this door!" Her ears rang as his voice boomed around the small room. He hammered on the door again. "Anyone out there? We're stuck in here!"

Chapter Thirteen

Her phone was dead. Again. If he wasn't so stressed, he'd think it funny how often she forgot to charge her phone. It was so…un-Jade-like.

He prayed someone needed something from the closet soon. He couldn't bear to think about being stuck in here until the end of the show, or worse, tomorrow morning when the cleaning crew showed up to put everything back in order. Certainly he'd be missed before then. His performance part of the show was done but still, it was *his* show. Someone would get worried. Several people knew he'd gone to look for something in the costume closet. Eventually they'd come looking. Wouldn't they? *They would.* He wasn't an insignificant child, he was a superstar. *He mattered.*

He hammered on the door again, but with the chaos and noise of the program, he was pretty sure someone needed to be walking by in order to hear it. He swore violently and gave the door a kick. Not as hard as he wanted to, but damaging his leg kicking a metal door wasn't a good idea. He turned around and slithered to the floor. That elevator episode had been bad, but this was worse. It was a *closet.* And filled up with so much crap it seemed like the walls were closing in on him. He tugged at his shirt collar, and Jade's voice sounded a long way off when she spoke.

"Han, are you going to be okay? You look like you

might pass out. Or throw up."

He'd neither the strength nor the desire to pretend with her. The meltdown he had in the elevator was mild compared to what he was feeling now. He covered his ears with his palms and squeezed his eyes shut in an effort to block out the sights and sounds rising up from the past. It barely registered when Jade sat next to him and rubbed his arm. What happened to all the air?

"I need to get out. *Get me out.*"

He opened his eyes, and Jade was on her knees in front of him. He quickly shut them again. Looking at her made him feel things he didn't want to feel, things he couldn't deal with.

She pulled his hands away from his ears and put hers on his cheeks. "Open your eyes and look at me, Han."

That voice. That wonderful voice. He could do nothing but obey. His vision was filled with the most gorgeous eyes he'd ever looked into. Jade's eyes. A plethora of emotions swirled around in them, but what struck him hardest was the concern. *For him.* No one ever looked at him like that. Not even Marguerite. He knew she'd cared about him, but so much of what she felt centered around his talent, his gift. She had cared about that more than she had cared about him as a person, as a child who was alone and desperate. A child running from a world filled with indifference and hoping to find someone who thought he mattered. And he *had* mattered to her. But not in a way he truly needed, and certainly not the way Jade's expression told him he mattered to her.

"Han, focus on *me*. Listen to *me*. You're going to be okay. The air in here is not going to run out.

Everything is going to be fine. We *will* get out. You need to take some deep breaths and try to calm down."

Sweat drenched his body, and he began to tremble deep inside. He took a breath in through his nose and let it out slowly, but it didn't help. In that moment, he realized he was dealing with more than just his claustrophobia. In less than a week, everything Jade had given him, was giving him right now, would be gone. Just like everyone else in his life he cared about. The important people always left. His mother. His brother. Marguerite. Now Jade. He clenched his teeth as anger flashed through him. He wasn't supposed to feel like this about Jade. He had decided. So that couldn't be it. It must be because he wasn't able to get her out of his system the way he did every other woman he desired.

He groaned and closed his eyes. He didn't want to look at her right now. What her eyes were telling him was too much to cope with on top of his claustrophobia. Every single piece of him ached and throbbed for her.

Then her lips were on his. Soft and tender and filled with so much more than lust. The fire was there. The fire was always there. But it was the rest that tied his gut in knots and had so many sensations and emotions exploding in him at once he couldn't control them. Most of them buried for so long he no longer had the strength to keep them down.

He wrapped his hands around her arms and set her away from him. "No. It's too much. I can't do it. I can't think about it." He put his hands on either side of his head. Maybe if he squeezed hard enough, the memories, the feelings, the needs would all go back down, deep down inside where they belonged.

"Han. Please let me help you. What do you need

me to do to help you cope?"

He dropped his hands in defeat, his gaze frantically moving over her. He wanted to kiss her, touch her, feel her writhing under him so he couldn't think about anything else. It overwhelmed him, and the strength to fight his demons vanished like a wisp of smoke. Whatever defenses kept them at bay, Jade's concern, her unselfish desire to help him with nothing in it for herself, to give him *whatever* he needed, whether it was best for her or not, obliterated them. Desperation set in. Because the one thing he could think of to make him forget, he couldn't ask of her. The mere thought of using her to satisfy his own selfish desires turned his stomach. The fact he'd used women in that way his whole life turned his stomach. Even though they'd used him right back. Even though he made sure they knew the score before he got involved with them.

Looking at this woman kneeling in front of him, eager to give him whatever she could to help him, left him disgusted with himself. When had he seen her do anything but give of herself? She'd gone against her instincts to give her sister the kind of wedding she wanted. She'd gone out of her comfort zone repeatedly to perform at his benefit in order to help children desperately in need of it. What had he ever done to deserve what she was offering right now?

He looked over her shoulder, ashamed to look her in the eye any longer. *Big mistake.* He could've sworn the room shrank right before his eyes. Whether he deserved her help or not, he needed it. He didn't dare think about having to spend an entire night locked in here. Was it possible that keeping everything locked inside him, never voicing it to anyone, made it larger than it really was? Could talking about it make it go away forever? Or maybe, telling *her* would make her realize there was nothing she *could* do. Letting him screw her would certainly help the here and now, but since she told him she didn't want a fling—and he wasn't willing to ask it of her—he decided she needed to know just how ugly his life had been. Maybe then she would back off and *leave him alone* so he could pull the pieces of this life back together. But the thought of her actually doing that made his head explode. The here and now receded, and he emotionally vomited all over her. Alejandro Rivera, Devil of the Dance Floor, was gone and only five-year-old Alejandro remained.

He pulled his knees to his chest and wrapped his arms around them. "I need you to listen to me, Jade. I need to tell you what happened so you'll understand why I can't give you what you want. What you deserve.

"I was five when it happened. I was so sick of that pimp banging on our door, because every time he did, *Mamá* told us to hide in the closet and be quiet, even though we already knew what to do. Whenever a man came to the door, we had to stay in the closet, no matter what we heard, until she told us it was okay to come out. That last time was the worst. I was so scared. He wouldn't stop screaming at her. I don't know if he was throwing things, throwing her, or both. *Mamá* was crying and talking so fast I couldn't understand what she was saying."

He swallowed and squeezed his eyes shut. *He was such a baby.* But he needed to say it. Jade had to know the kind of person he really was. To see he didn't deserve the help she was trying to give him.

"Javier, he was the brave one. He kept whispering to me that everything would be fine. As long as we stayed there and kept quiet, everything would work out okay. We had to be patient. Javier said he wanted to get out of the closet too, and help *Mamá,* but he wasn't going to because *Mamá* knew what was best.

"I wasn't brave like Javier. I didn't want to help; I wanted to get out and run as far away as I could. I didn't want *una madre* who had men over every night, a mother who made us spend so much time hiding in the closet. I wanted a real family like my friend Raul. I wanted to get out of there, go to Raul's house and never come back."

He rested his forehead on his knees for a moment and took a deep breath. He wanted to laugh at himself in disgust. Was he still that same scared little boy? Afraid to say it out loud? He lifted his head.

"But I was too scared to move." He clenched his jaw in an effort to hold the words back, but they tumbled out anyway, his voice harsh. "I hated her, Jade. I hated my mother."

He took a deep shuddering breath, trying to relieve the feeling of suffocation. Though surprised what a relief it was to finally say it out loud, he'd said enough. He felt like a deflated balloon with nothing left inside and had no desire to talk about it anymore, to think about it anymore. And he certainly didn't want to feel like *this* about Jade anymore.

Why didn't she say anything? Was she disgusted with him now? She should be.

Then he looked into her eyes and everything started bubbling up again. Maybe being in this closet had tipped him over the edge and his sanity with it. He hadn't been so out of control since that fateful night. After that, being in control was his obsession, his goal, his number one priority. Control of his body, his environment, his women, his *emotions*. And now it was finally biting him in the butt. He could only hold the lid on for so long before it left him where he was right now. In control of *nothing*. He couldn't even get himself to move. Exactly like that night.

"*Mamá* screamed." He put his hands over his ears again, realized what he was doing and instead balled them into fists and put them on his knees. Almost thirty years later and he could still hear it echoing in his head. "Then everything went silent. I don't know how long the silence lasted before we heard someone moving around. The angry voices were gone, but worse, there weren't any voices at all. We waited and waited and *waited* for *Mamá* to tell us we could come out. It was so hard. I couldn't breathe. I wanted to run, but I couldn't move. Javier went to sleep after a while, but I couldn't. Someone was out there. It had to be *Mamá*. Why wouldn't she let us out? The closet was dark and *so* small. I could've sworn we were running out of air, and I started to get dizzy. I kept trying to breath, but it only made me dizzier until I finally passed out. I don't know how long it was before Javier woke me up, telling me it was time to get out because something was wrong."

His mouth snapped shut when he realized he was speaking Spanish. Had he been speaking it the whole time? Did Jade know enough Spanish to understand him? He looked at her. Were there even any English words left in his head? He forced himself to open his hands and wrapped his arms around his legs. Somehow it felt better to hug his knees to his chest. Like it protected him from…everything.

"It's okay, Han. Tell me the rest. You need to. You'll feel better for it, and I won't tell anyone what happened to you."

She had understood, had spoken in Spanish as well. What had he done to deserve such a woman in his life? He hadn't believed they existed beyond the fiction of books and movies. She put her hand on his, where it was wrapped around his legs. Warmth and peace flooded him with the gesture. Whether or not he needed to say the words was irrelevant. He could no longer keep them in.

"*Mamá* was so still at first I thought she was sleeping. That she forgot we were in the closet and went to bed. Javier had my hand and was pulling me behind him, so he got to the bed first. I didn't see much before he turned around and wouldn't let me get any closer. But I'd seen enough. All the blood. She was dead. Beat to a pulp by her pimp. He'd laid her on the bed, straightened up the place and left. Javier said if he found out we had been there when he killed her and knew it was him, he'd kill us too. So we grabbed some clothes, all the food and money we could find, and left. I don't even know if the police ever caught her killer."

Then Jade's arms were around him, his head pressed into her chest, and her hand rubbed his back as though he was still that scared little boy. He stiffened. He didn't need her sympathy, her *pity*. All he'd needed was to say it out loud. For someone else to know. Still, though he hated to admit it, the human contact, her genuine concern for him, helped. He may have helped to free her from her own fears with his dance lessons, but she'd freed him as well, from his past. A calmness settled over him as he rested there soaking up the tenderness she showered on him, something he'd needed since his mother died, though he hadn't realized how powerful it could be until she gave it to him. A soothing balm to his broken soul.

He took a long, deep, cleansing breath before he pulled away. Suddenly he felt all kinds of stupid. Did he really have so little backbone getting locked in a closet made him say things he never wanted to talk about, never wanted to say to *anyone*? He was an idiot. People didn't want to know about your ghosts, to listen to sad stories about your childhood.

Before the silence had a chance to get awkward, someone unlocked the door and opened it. Barely able to control his panic to get out, he shoved Jade away from him and scrambled to his feet. He didn't bother with niceties, just pushed his way past the person who opened the door and bolted out. All he could think about was getting out of the building to breathe some fresh air before he could return to overseeing the program.

The rest of the show went by in a blur, but he liked that it kept him too busy to think. About anything. And though he told Jade he wanted her to stay for all of it, he knew she left. And the fact he could instinctively know she was gone made him twitchy. Why did she have to have this effect on him? His life was perfect before she came along. He had everything he could possibly want. Fame, money, looks, a kickass body, and a new business that would keep him in the dance world long after his body no longer could. It was all he'd ever wanted. Needed even. Now *she* had him wanting things he decided long ago he *didn't* want. Or need.

Damn her. He had no use for a woman's arms around him, giving him things he hadn't known he needed and asking for nothing in return. She filled a hole in his soul he'd been perfectly content to leave empty, and in the process left a gaping one elsewhere which had him aching inside and out. He didn't need this. Didn't *want* this. Had made damn sure he never got within a mile of *this* with the women in his life. Thank goodness it was less than a week until the wedding. One more rehearsal, the wedding day and he could be done with her. Could concentrate his efforts on coping with the new hole a *woman* had carved out of him.

****

Han was different, but she couldn't put her finger on how.

He was a bear at rehearsal, but she didn't think it was that. After all, he was the Devil of the Dance Floor. She'd seen that side of him plenty. No, it was something else. It didn't help that her stomach sank every time she tried to figure it out. Not that it really mattered in the end. A few more hours and he would be, for all intents and purposes, out of her life. She didn't know which hurt more. That he didn't want to give her the relationship she needed, or that he couldn't. And she still had to figure out a way to live without him.

It certainly didn't help that they were a couple for the entire wedding, so he was always *there*. Walking with her down the aisle. Sitting next to her at the bridal table, posing for pictures with her. Or that the wedding, thanks to Beck's generosity, was a fairytale come true. It left her feeling like *she* was living a fairytale. And she wasn't even the one getting married.

The expensive designer dress not only looked good on her but made her feel good about herself. She was partnered for the day with none other than Alejandro Rivera *in a tuxedo.* And the backdrop for it all: the historic Greystone Mansion, a castle fit for any girl's dream.

For Jade, the best part was that she did it all without her locket. It didn't fit with the look Lexi was going for, but rather than being anxious without it, she felt free. For the first time she was actually *living* her life, being the person she was supposed to be. She hadn't once reached for the locket to find it missing, and she had Han to thank for helping her over that final hurdle.

When the time for the wedding party dance arrived, she decided to live in the moment and enjoy the fantasy. Nothing like this would happen to her again, and she wasn't going to ruin it by worrying about the emotional quagmire of the future. She deserved a fairytale day just as much as Lexi. Han wasn't going to spoil it because he wasn't her Prince Charming. She'd pretend he was and savor every moment. She was grateful for all he'd given her, as well as her sister. So screw the future; she'd deal with reality later. The reality of nailing their dance was enough right now. All the hard work and emotional turmoil had been worth it. The satisfaction of having silenced a roomful of wedding guests with their dancing, of getting it just right, was well worth the time and effort they put in. Still, after they left the dance floor, she collapsed in her chair with relief and fanned herself.

"You did it, Jade." Han smiled slightly and raised

his brows "How does it feel?"

She fiddled with her linen napkin for a moment. Good question. How did it feel? She closed her eyes, the white noise of a room full of wedding guests eating, talking, and laughing filled her head for a moment. "It feels...wonderful. Liberating. I understand better now, why you do it."

He smiled again, but it didn't quite reach his eyes. "*Sí.* Is good, no? I am proud of you, Jade. You've come a long way from where you were two months ago, and your dancing today was beyond anything I hoped to accomplish."

"I should be thanking *you*. Because of you, I've been able to lay the last few of my ghosts to rest. I could never repay you for that."

"I don't expect you to. Believe it or not, I enjoyed the process."

He leaned back in his chair and shifted his gaze over her shoulder then back to her. "*Damn,* what is it with that guy? He's walked through the room twice that I've seen and had his eyes glued to you each time. It looks like he works here, but I haven't seen him actually *working.* I'm tempted to go ask him what his problem is. He's old enough to be your father for God's sake."

She turned in her chair to see who he was referring to but didn't find anyone that looked like the man he described. "I don't see any old men in a Greystone Mansion uniform."

He shook his head. "Never mind. He left."

She unclenched a hand she hadn't realized was balled into a fist until that moment and searched the crowd for Lexi. Whoever it was Han had seen, she didn't need it ruining her sister's day. Her heart slowed its thunderous pace when her eyes landed on her sister's laughing face. She frowned momentarily and suppressed a shiver. Why was she so worked up about a possible gatecrasher? Because the only old man she could think of who would be interested in her was her stepfather?

"What is it Jade? You've gone white as a sheet."

"Nothing." She swallowed the desire to vomit and crossed her arms over her stomach. "Just me being stupid. Ignore it."

His brows drew together in a frown, then his jaw clenched for a moment before he nodded his head. "Will do."

She laughed, and her tension eased. "The only old man I could think of who'd be looking at me is Gene Murray. I freaked myself out."

He nodded, and an indecisive look momentarily crossed his face. "Why didn't you press charges for what that bastard did to you?"

"Han…" She squeezed her eyes shut for a moment. "This isn't the place. I don't want to discuss my stepfather at Lexi's wedding."

He ran a hand around the back of his neck. "You're right. And it's not like I have a right to that sort of information anyway."

Shoot. Now she wanted him to know. "I think it was mostly because it was so out of character from the man I'd known for years. I really think grief and alcohol changed him. He'd been good to my mother. Loved her. And after the mess she'd been through with my biological father, she deserved some happiness. I felt like it would taint her memory in some way if I went after him. When it comes down to it, he really didn't do more than some inappropriate touching. Besides, I didn't have much of case against him. It would have been my word against his."

He reached out and took her hand in both of his. "Lexi didn't know it was going on at the time?"

She shook her head. "She was never around. I think he made sure of it. And I'm glad. She knows now, but not then."

"So he didn't try anything with her?"

"Nope. Thank God. She's assured me of that."

"This may be highly inappropriate, and it probably isn't the time or the place, but aren't you worried about there being other victims?"

She looked down at their joined hands and nodded her head. "I was. At first."

"Why not now?"

"Jolene and Ben—the family friends that gave us a place to live and left me the business when they died—helped put my mind at rest about it. They knew something bad had happened and after some time had passed, I was able to tell Jolene why I didn't want to live with my stepfather, why I didn't want Lexi anywhere near him. Not that I gave her any details, but enough she knew we shouldn't be around him. They hired a private detective to keep tabs on him. He never did anything else suspicious. Was never seen in the company of another female, much less teenage girls. I was content to get away and put the past behind me. Which included some lengthy therapy." She bit her lip. "I really don't want to be thinking about him today of all days."

He let go of her hand. "Time to change the subject.

Would you like me to get you something from the bar?"

She started to refuse the offer, then thought better of it. Taking the edge off with a drink might be just the thing. Gene Murray had taken enough. He wasn't going to ruin this special day.

"Gin and tonic sounds perfect."

He raised his brows. "Our evening at The Conga Room didn't start you down the wrong path, did it?"

She laughed softly. "Geez, what kind of impression do you have of me? That wasn't the first time I'd ever had alcohol, *amigo.* I was drinking at dinner the night we met, remember? It was just the first time I'd had enough to get buzzed."

He winked, and her heart squeezed at the momentary return of the old Han. "Just making sure. One gin and tonic coming right up."

As she waited for Han, her eyes rested on Lexi. Her little sister was happy and heading off to a new chapter of her life. One that Jade now played a different role in. Part of her was sad she no longer had a little sister to care for, but a bigger part was happy. Lexi was starting life with a man who was as crazy about her as she was about him, and although their journey to get there hadn't been an easy one, the difficulties made it all the more precious. Jade was now free to do and go wherever she wanted whenever she chose. She and Lexi could now be true sisters. What a glorious feeling.

She looked across the room at Han as he waited his turn at the bar and saw he was talking with a woman obviously having a fan girl moment. Not that she blamed her because, truth be told, not long ago she would've been guilty of the same thing had she run into him standing in line, rather than in a broken elevator.

Her thoughts were brought back to the present when a waiter set something on the table next to her. A man just invaded her personal space, and it didn't faze her. A small smile pulled at her lips as she looked down at her empty dinner plate and saw a folded piece of paper next to it. What in the world? She picked it up and opened it.

Jade,

I'm sorry to intrude on Alexa's special day but couldn't pass up the opportunity to apologize for the way I treated you after your mother died. I understand if you can't forgive me, but you have to know how deeply I regret everything I did. If I could go back and change things I would.

Gene Murray

She folded the paper and set it back on the table as Han set her drink in front of her and then sat down. She picked it up and took a healthy swig, trying to discern exactly what she was feeling. Like alcohol could somehow make her think more clearly. What an idiot. She breathed deeply before she took another swallow.

"What the hell happened while I was gone?" he growled, reached out a hand towards her, then put it on the table and balled it into a fist.

Pain darted through her at his unwillingness to touch her now. The man with touching OCD. She took a deep breath, started to speak, then cleared her throat and tried again. "My stepfather gave me a letter of apology."

He swore in Spanish under his breath. "So that's why that old man kept looking at you."

"Most likely." She shook her head. "I'm trying to decide if running after the jerk and confronting him is a good idea. I don't want to ruin Lexi's day. She's so happy, and she doesn't know our stepfather is here."

He nodded. "Are you afraid to be alone around him?"

"That, too. But I *so* want to tell him how he ruined my life for so long. He shouldn't be allowed to get away with sending me an apology and thinking everything is fine now."

He reached out his hand towards her fist as it rested on the table near her drink, then picked up his drink and swirled the ice around in it. "If I had the opportunity to tell my *mamá* how she ruined my life with her choices, I would. I'll go with you so you don't have to face him alone. Lexi doesn't need to know. She can think we're sneaking off together."

Jade's eyes filled with tears as she looked at him, saw his worried expression. He had her back if she needed him. She didn't want to miss this opportunity and regret it for the rest of her life, so she jumped to her feet. "Let's do it."

He stood too and put his arm around her waist, directing her towards the balcony doors. So now he wanted to touch her? She bit back a frustrated growl. She needed to stop worrying about where his hands were and get used to them not being on her. After today, his touch would be a thing of the past.

He bent his head and whispered in her ear. "We'll act like we're going outside for a little fun, so Lexi doesn't know anything is wrong." His arm tightened and pulling her close, he nibbled on her neck.

Her throat closed up with emotion, and all she managed was a nod as heat from his caress fizzed through her. When they were outside, she sucked in a breath on a hiss and halted in her tracks when she saw her stepfather making his way across the grounds. Her first look at him in almost a decade. All of a sudden confronting him didn't seem like a good idea. She could barely look at the man without wanting to run screaming in the other direction. "Han—"

His hand tightened around her waist. "Don't lose courage now. You're strong, Jade, I've seen it. You can do this. I'll make sure he doesn't get away with saying or doing anything that makes you uncomfortable. You need this."

She turned and buried her face in Han's shoulder. She may be strong, but this was one demon she didn't want to face. Especially not today. Just seeing the man was putting her in a tailspin, much less actually talking to him. Truth be told, he had more power to hurt her than she him. Telling him off would accomplish nothing more than getting her all wound up. She grabbed the lapel of Han's jacket and balled her fist. Tears filled her eyes, and she squeezed them shut as her breath caught in her throat. She forced herself to let it out slowly. To concentrate on making herself relax. To not let her emotions get the better of her. She focused on the steady beat of Han's heart as she rested her head against his chest.

What do you know? Being in Han's embrace worked the same magic as her locket. She took in another deep breath and let it out slowly, savoring the glorious scent that was Han. Han, who'd helped her to a better, brighter future, whether or not he ended up being part of it. She pulled away and looked up into topaz eyes that would forever haunt her dreams, and they were filled with concern. For her. He may have spent the day pretending he didn't care about her, but he *did*. It may not be what she wanted and needed from him, but she did affect him on more than a sexual level. Whether he liked it or not.

She licked her lips, suddenly thirsty as the warmth of the summer sun beat down on her. All she wanted was to go back inside where it was cool, and life was about happy things. "I've changed my mind. I don't want to do this. What's the point? Anything I say would never affect his life the way he affected mine. Abandoning him the way we did and never speaking to him again is the biggest statement I could make. The fact he wishes he could go back and change what he did means it's been eating away at him all these years. I hope his guilt gives him an ulcer. No reaction to his apology seems like pretty good payback to me."

His brows drew together, a troubled expression on his face. "But what about closure? Don't you think confronting him would bring a sense of closure for you that could help? Letting him know exactly what the consequences of his actions were."

"Closure?" She shrugged. "It isn't all it's cracked up to be, Han. I really think the best kind of closure for me is not letting what he did affect the way I live my life from here on out. Forgetting him and moving on is my best closure. Why would I want to waste any more emotion on someone like him, when I could be spending my time enjoying someone like you?" She smiled and ran a finger lightly down his cheek, reveling in the feel of his five-o'clock shadow on her fingertip. Enjoying touching someone was all the closure she needed. "Let's get back to the reception before we miss the cutting of the cake. The best part of a wedding reception is the cake."

Han chuckled and dropped his arms from around her, taking her by the hand and turning around to head back inside. "No doubt."

When she looked at Han's smiling face, into eyes where the smile didn't quite reach, some of her joy faded. Still, Gene Murray was well and truly in her past, that chapter of her life closed for good.

After he helped her back into her seat and sat down next to her, she realized she'd forgotten to ask him how things were going with Cat. The week up to the wedding had been so hectic, she hadn't asked what happened with her after the fundraiser.

"How's Cat? Did she enjoy being on stage?"

He nodded and this time the smile did reach his eyes. "If you ask me, she's going to be a superstar. She's received several offers since the show, and it's only been a week. I told her to take her time and decide what's best for her, and that I'll help her in whatever way she needs me to."

"Pay it forward?"

He shrugged. "Partly. But mostly I like the kid and want her to have a better life."

"I told her to get in touch with me if she needed anything, but something just occurred to me. If she wants to get out of East L.A., I'd love to have her stay with me until she figures out what she wants to do. Lexi's room has been empty for a while now."

He narrowed his eyes at her for a moment. "I don't know Jade. That's a lot to take on. She's a pretty messed up kid. Maybe you should think about it for a while and let me know if you still want to do it."

"She may be a bit messed up, but she's got her

head on straight. If she wants to pursue a future in dance, I want to help her do it. Tell her, Han."

He nodded. "All right then, I will. But after that, leave me out of it. I'm not going to be your middle man."

"I wouldn't want you to."

Chapter Fourteen

"You look like hell."

Beck swung open the door to his house and indicated with his head for him to come in.

Han suppressed a scowl as he crossed the threshold. "You look the complete opposite. Marriage agrees with you, even after a month of living in the real world."

"I'm thinking a drink is in order. Shall we head to the man cave?"

"Sure." Han moved in that direction. Whether he cracked open a beer or not, the man cave was where they automatically went when he visited his friend. "Drinking hasn't helped, though. I've tried."

He followed Beck through the house to a room that was most definitely a man cave. Pool table, recliners, large screen TV, a well-stocked bar, refrigerator. He threw himself into a recliner and made himself comfortable.

"However, it might make it easier to say what I have to say." He winced. He needed liquid courage now?

"Pick your poison."

"Whatever you're having works for me."

Beck took two bottles of beer out of the fridge, handed one to Han and sat down in the matching recliner, both of which faced a massive flat-panel television hanging on the wall.

"Wanna watch the game?"

Han took a long swig of beer and shrugged a shoulder carelessly. "What the hell."

Three beers and a quarter of a football game later, Beck finally addressed the elephant in the room. "This is about Jade."

Han tensed. "What makes you say that?"

"Only a woman can make a man look like he's drowning with no hope of a life preserver." Beck finished off his beer and gave Han a wicked smile. "The Devil of the Dance Floor has been cast into the fires of Hell. It's about time."

"Screw you."

"No thanks. I have Lexi for that. Thank God."

"Damn." He took a long swig of his beer.

"Why are you here, Han? I'm pretty sure it's not for my company."

He shrugged and ran a hand around the back of his neck. "How did you know Lexi was worth taking a risk on? Weren't you worried she would screw you over in one way or another?"

"With the example my parents set? Hell, yes."

"So why did you get involved with her in the first place? We used to be love 'em and leave 'em buddies, bailing each other out when a woman got too clingy."

"I had no choice."

"Has she ever got you by the balls."

Beck shrugged. "That isn't it at all. I didn't want to love her. I didn't want her to have that kind of hold over me. So I fought it every step of the way. Then I realized it felt a hell of a lot better giving in, giving myself over to her, and was totally worth taking the risk of losing it all someday. That's not to say it's all heavenly bliss. She's hurt me. I've definitely hurt her. It's what you do afterward that counts. Hurting with her by my side is ten times better than hurting because she's not there. Part of the commitment we made to each other was that we'd stick together when things get tough and find a way to work through it together."

Han let loose several Spanish expletives under his breath, and Beck laughed.

"Need another beer?"

"I could use a lot more than the three I've had. Give me two."

"Might as well admit it, *ese,* it's over. You can never go back now."

"Whatever. Something else gone screwy I can thank my mother for. Maybe I should stop letting her run my life from the grave."

Beck raised his beer. "I'll drink to that. Here's to our mothers, may they forever rot in hell."

Han clinked his bottle on Beck's in hearty agreement.

****

Chica need ur help with my business accounts. B there in a few. Sí?

No…No, no, *no*. She could *not* do this. She'd finally come to terms with the fact she loved a man she could never have and now he wanted her to work for him. Not. Gonna. Happen.

OMG. R u stalking me?

She slammed a palm on her forehead. Why did she answer him? She groaned and covered her face with her hands as she threw herself back on the couch. It didn't help that his timing sucked in epic proportions. She was at that very moment watching a recording of him. Yeah, she was a mess. Physically and emotionally. Her house was a mess too. For the first time in her life. She had to stop him from coming over. Frantically she typed on her phone.

Not a good time.

Right as she hit send there was a bang on the door.

She swore in Spanish. Somehow it didn't seem as foul that way. And fewer people knew she was doing it. *Thanks a lot, Han.*

Go away and leave me alone.

As soon as she hit send she realized what a bad move that was. Now he knew she was home. She sighed in resignation. Her house was a mess. Her hair was a mess. She was wearing pajamas in the middle of the day, and Alejandro Rivera was dancing on her television set. That pretty much summed up the story of her life.

She picked up the remote and gave the off button a violent push. Maybe if he saw her like this he'd leave her alone. As long as he didn't find out he was the reason for it...She yanked the door open, making sure her expression and her posture told him how *un*happy she was to see him.

He leaned nonchalantly against the door frame, but something in his eyes said he wasn't as relaxed as he appeared. "I see I also taught you some new Spanish. And you're looking lovely as usual. Can I come in?"

"No. It's my day off. I don't have time for a new client anyway. You'll have to find someone else."

"I've tried. You're the only one for me, *chica.*"

"Not falling for your charm, Alejandro."

"Not going anywhere until you let me in, Jade."

She ground her teeth and stepped back as she swung the door wide, making a sweeping motion with her arm. "Whatever it takes to get you to leave, I guess."

"I see you haven't lost your charm. What the hell happened in here? Where's the real Jade and what have you done with her? Have you been sick?"

Feigning unconcern, she shrugged as she closed the door, walked across the room and sat back down on the couch, not bothering to offer him a seat, hoping he'd take the hint and be quick. "I've turned over a new leaf."

He ignored her rudeness and sat on the couch next to her. Damn him and his OCD. He was going to touch her, she just knew it, and if he did, she may very well fall apart in front of him. She was *so* not ready for this.

"You're going to have to hire another accountant. I'm not available."

"I lied. After you showed me what was going on, I was able to figure out the rest. I hired another accountant to straighten things out with the IRS."

He picked up a strand of her hair and just the brush of his finger on her arm as he did it was too much.

"I'm not sleeping with you."

He raised a brow. "I can't get your hair out of my mind, which is crazy because I have never been interested in blondes until I met you. In fact, had we not been forced into each other's company, I never would've looked twice at you."

"You have *such* a way with words. How do you do it?"

He chuckled and dropped the strand. "You have no idea how often I've imagined what your hair would look like draped across my naked body. And yours."

She'd meant what she said sarcastically, but suddenly it was all too true. She tried to block out the word picture he created, because as much as she wanted to see what he described, live and in person, she wasn't going to open herself up to that kind of pain. She wanted a real relationship with a real man and if she let things go any farther than they had with Han, he could ruin her forever.

"Since you didn't hear the first time, I. Am. Not. Sleeping. With. You." He ran a finger down her cheek, and she couldn't suppress a shiver. "Back off."

"The personal space bubble is up and running, I see."

She ignored him. What was she supposed to say? *No, it feels so good I may never get enough if you touch me again.* Her space bubble was gone, non-existent where he was concerned. The last thing she wanted him to know was how *well* his charm worked on her.

"Never in my life have I seen skin like yours. You have no idea how many times I've dreamed about what my hands would look like on it as they touched you— *everywhere*."

She barely managed to stifle a whimper. She'd never wanted anything as much as she wanted Han to do that right there and then.

"Han, stop it! Just—stop. I'm not going to let you ruin my life for a few moments of pleasure. Besides, I have too much baggage for you. I'm so far beyond not-a-quick-lay for you."

"Like you've ruined me?"

"What is *that* supposed to mean? How in the world could I possibly have ruined Alejandro Rivera?"

"After what my mother put me through, I decided I wasn't going to love another woman. She made my life miserable before and after she died. Then, when I lost my brother—it was the nail in the coffin. Loving hurt too much and I wasn't going to let it happen anymore. Not even with Marguerite. I cared about her and she cared about me, but a lot of it was based on what we could do for each other. She was my friend and I am very grateful for everything she did for me. When she died, it hurt. But not a gut-wrenching, clear to the bones kind of pain you feel when someone you love is gone. It was enough, though, to reinforce my decision to not care about a woman for any more than what they can do for me."

Her gut twisted at his words. Like it had when he told her what happened to him as a child. Every time she thought about it, her heart bled for those poor little boys. She hardened her heart. Just like he needed to protect *his* heart, she had to protect *hers*. From him.

"Han, you have to stop. I want you to leave. I refuse to do this with you. Please." Her voiced hitched, and she paused for a moment to regain her composure. "Don't ignore what I want like my stepfather did." Her voice was barely above a whisper. She didn't like comparing him to her stepfather, but it felt like the same kind of pressure. A man forcing her to do something she didn't want because *he* wanted it.

"Hell!" he muttered under his breath, and jumped to his feet, running his hands through his hair as he paced across the room. He stopped in front of the Picasso print, clasped his hands behind his back and stared at it like it was talking to him. Softly, yet violently he said, "Do *not* compare me to that bastard

ever again."

"Tell me, Han, what was that little speech about the women in your life for, if not to compare *me* to *them?*"

He muttered some Spanish expletives, and she smiled. This was the Han she wanted to see. The real one. Not the smooth-talker who walked in her door a few minutes ago.

"I'll tell you why I was comparing you, why I came over here, though I'm starting to think it was a waste of time and emotion. You're a real piece of work."

"I seem to remember hearing that before. Get to the point and be on your way."

He strode back across the room and stopped in front of her, his chest heaving like he'd danced around the room first. Before she realized his intention, he grabbed her by the upper arms and hauled her to her feet. "I love you, Jade. More than I've loved anyone. More than I love dancing. So much, I want to marry you right this instant so no other man can have you. So no other man can possess you like I need to possess you. So no other man can enjoy your body the way it deserves to be enjoyed. And I swore on my mother I would *never* give a woman that kind of power over me. *That* is what I came here to tell you." He dropped his hands and stepped back a pace. "And since you've made it abundantly clear you don't want me around, I'll leave you to your life."

He had his hand on the doorknob before she had the wherewithal to say something.

"Han! No! Please. Don't go." Her voice broke, and she swallowed the giant lump in her throat. There was no way she could let him leave after that, so she said the only thing she could think of that would keep him there. "I love you, too."

He dropped his hand and slowly turned around. "You know if it was anyone else saying that, I wouldn't believe them. Right now, the only thing I'm having a hard time believing is that you actually said it. You actually feel the same."

She moved towards him as he was talking, and he walked towards her. When they met in the middle of the room, he took her in his arms and buried his face in her neck.

"What do you mean?" she whispered.

He lifted his head, linked his hands in the small of her back and leaned away from her slightly. His internal battle showed clearly on his face and as she waited for him to speak, she realized he was trembling. It was a rather humbling discovery—that she could make such a man quiver in her arms. She actually had Alejandro Rivera, *the man she'd just watched dancing on television,* shaking in his shoes. Simply because she loved him. If she thought about it anymore, her head would probably explode.

He placed his forehead on hers and closed his eyes. "I mean, that someone as amazing as you could love *me*. Han. Not Alejandro, the boy who could dance like there was no tomorrow, not Alejandro Rivera, The Devil of the Dance Floor. Just me, for me. I've always thought that person was unlovable. Take away my talent and I'm not worth bothering with."

"Oh, Han." She choked on her words. Took a deep breath. It hurt that he felt that way about himself. He was an incredible human being and she was determined to do everything in her power to make sure he not only knew she felt that way but believed it about himself. "Here and now, I am dedicating myself to making sure you never feel that way again."

His tension melted away, his arms tightened and he lifted his head to look her in the eyes. "See, *chica*. How could I not love you?"

She wrapped her arms around him and hugged him hard, burying her head in his chest, swamped with the need to be as close to him as humanly possible, imprinting the feel of him on her flesh. Holding the little boy inside him tight in an effort to give him a sense of security he never had.

"My dear, *dear* Alejandro, I'm never going to let you go. I'm going to prove to you love is worth the risk. Together we can create the family you always wanted. The family you deserve."

"Ah, *mi amor, mi angel,* I hope you are right with all my heart." He tenderly took hold of her chin and tilted her face to him. All noise faded away but for the sound of her heart pounding in her ears as he looked at her, his eyes swirling with emotions she hadn't dared dream any man would have for her, much less *this* man.

The arm around her waist held her tightly against him as he lowered his lips to hers and kissed her with reverence. Her head spun, her heart thumped slow and hard. This man, this incredible, talented, sexy, aggravating man was treating her like *she* mattered, like what *she* wanted was more important than his desires. And having a man like that touch her was the most glorious thing in the world.

"Jade, you need to know, I'm aware our physical union has to happen slowly, and I assure you, I'm willing to do or not do whatever you feel comfortable with. You don't have to be afraid there will be some point where I can't stop. If at any time you don't want to do anything, all you have to do is tell me."

She sighed and nodded her head once, fighting the urge to pinch herself to make sure this was really happening. She must have done something right somewhere along the line that a man like him would be willing to deal with any physical inhibitions she might have because of her past.

"I love you so much. I can hardly wrap my head around the fact this is real. That you love me that much."

He laughed softly. "*Chica,* I feel exactly the same about you. How could I not be willing to do whatever it takes to make you happy?"

He stepped back from her, running a hand down her arm and taking hold of her hand. With his free hand, he pulled the chain he wore around his neck out from under his t-shirt and unclasped it. Sliding the ring off, he placed it on her finger.

"Marguerite told me some day my soul mate would come along, and she wanted that woman to have her wedding ring. The ring she'd received from her soul mate. I never believed it would happen." He gave her a crooked smile. "I guess she was right after all."

"Oh, Han…It looks like an antique. It's beautiful. I feel so honored." She put the hand with the ring on it on his cheek and caressed his cheekbone with her thumb. "I'll treasure it, always."

He pulled her back in his arms, buried his face in her neck and promised, "As I will treasure you."

Would that voice always turn her bones to liquid? He took a nip of her neck, then whispered in her ear in

Spanish, half of which she couldn't translate because his breath in her ear and what he was doing with his hands made it impossible to think straight. Still, she understood enough it sent shivers down her spine.

"Han, you are such a *devil*!"

A word about the author...

Robyn Rychards grew up in the granola bowl of the United States—Boulder, Colorado, a town filled with fruits, flakes, and nuts. She considers herself a Jack-of-all-trades-master-of-none and has taught herself to sew, paint, play the piano, garden, cook, and the list goes on. But now that her books are published, she's thrilled to finally be considered a master of one. At least as much as a person can be, for the learning never really stops.

She feels her active imagination is a blessing and a curse, with the blessing far outweighing the curse, since it has led her to fulfill her dream of being a published romance author. Robyn started writing when she was a teenager because she didn't have enough books to read, and sometimes finds it hard to believe that people are willing to pay her to do something she enjoys so much. Then there's the added bonus of having a good reason to put off cooking and cleaning, much less a job that means you can stay in your jammies as long as you want. That's priceless.

Thank you for purchasing
this publication of The Wild Rose Press, Inc.

For questions or more information
contact us at
info@thewildrosepress.com.

The Wild Rose Press, Inc.
www.thewildrosepress.com

To visit with authors of
The Wild Rose Press, Inc.
join our yahoo loop at
http://groups.yahoo.com/group/thewildrosepress/

www.ingramcontent.com/pod-product-compliance
Lightning Source LLC
Chambersburg PA
CBHW060543260626
47161CB00003B/1033